About the Author

C S Whythe spent his childhood in Midlands Ireland. He received his higher education in London. He is the author of several guidebooks to travel and walking in Ireland, Spain and South America. His first novel, also published by Vanguard Press, "A Patina of Frost" was critically acclaimed. This is his second novel.

Waiting for the Feckin Corncrakes

C. S. Whythe

Waiting for the Feckin Corncrakes

Vanguard Press

VANGUARD PAPERBACK

© Copyright 2024
C. S. Whythe

The right of C. S. Whythe to be identified as author of
this work has been asserted by him in accordance with the
Copyright, Designs and Patents Act 1988.

All Rights Reserved

No reproduction, copy or transmission of this publication
may be made without written permission.
No paragraph of this publication may be reproduced,
copied or transmitted save with the written permission of the
publisher, or in accordance with the provisions
of the Copyright Act 1956 (as amended).

Any person who commits any unauthorised act in relation to
this publication may be liable to criminal
prosecution and civil claims for damages.

A CIP catalogue record for this title is
available from the British Library.

ISBN 978 1 83794 101 8

This is a work of fiction. Names, characters, businesses, places, events and incidents are either the product of the author's imagination or used in a fictitious manner. Any resemblance to actual persons, living or dead, or actual events is purely coincidental.

Vanguard Press is an imprint of
Pegasus Elliot Mackenzie Publishers Ltd.
www.pegasuspublishers.com

First Published in 2024

Vanguard Press
Sheraton House Castle Park
Cambridge England

Printed & Bound in Great Britain

For Birgit and Helen

The inspiration for this story comes from three extraordinary children, Owen, Liam and Clara

Peter

It is a cold, bleak February evening. The time of the year when the weather is marking time between the severity of winter and the dawn of spring. It's been one of those days that people from more stable climates snigger at – sunshine with squally showers. As dusk falls dark clouds are brooding, unsure whether to shower us with more water or just sit there threatening us. Thankfully the clouds will act as an insulating blanket during the night, ensuring that our windy island will be frost free. Tree buds, daffodils and crocuses are all poised to emerge but are apprehensive, reluctant to be pre-emptive, wanting reassurance that the winter frost has concluded.

Peter Sheridan is ascending the steps of The Cathedral of Christ the King in Mullingar. Our subject is tall, indeed, very tall, and very well dressed, and he strides smartly up the granite steps. He wears a full-length navy blue, Gaberdine coat, from the sleeves of which project black, leather gloves. His matching black, leather shoes are neatly polished. Beneath the dark grey, peaked hat his neck is adorned with a woollen red scarf. A man dressed properly. For Peter is going to the Saturday evening mass, and being properly dressed is cardinal. He always goes to the Saturday evening mass. Whenever it is on. Well, ever since the Church decreed that it fulfilled the obligation of mass on Sunday. User-friendly religion. Doubtless, those astute people in the Church thought it better to get the flock in on Saturdays, before they headed off to the pub. Then sore heads could sleep in on Sundays, and not come to the church to breathe alcohol fumes all over the priest when they opened their mouths to receive the blessed sacrament.

But this Saturday's mass is extra special. It's the first time he has been to the cathedral in months. The doors have been locked shut during the pandemic. Now, it should be noted that the government has not yet issued their diktat for the churches to reopen – they meet tonight to rubber-stamp the medical council's recommendation – but the dogs in the street know that they are about to, and our eager bishop, who cannot contain his frustration with them any longer (what body can assume the power to forbid people to come together to pray?) has invited his parishioners to mass this evening.

"We're not supposed to be here, y'know," Peter overhears one of the masked step ascenders mutter, "The ban has not yet been lifted. You saw what happened over Golfgate. Ministers resigning, because there was seventy of them at a dinner."

"Yeah but, a minister's one thing, a bishop an entirely different matter," is the reply, "you can go after a feckin minister, no problem, but who's goin to take on a bishop?"

Peter has several matters on his mind, some of them pressing issues he has to deal with, but right now he is really looking forward to being inside the cathedral after the long closure. One might say he is suffering from withdrawal symptoms. So much of his life has been passed in this great hall, from his baptism, through his first holy communion, then confirmation. Why, in his youth he attended two masses on a Sunday, the first for Holy Communion, and the second for the high mass when he would sing in the choir. Every component of the architecture of the building is familiar to him: the massive circular columns, the intricate mosaic floor, the golden gates into the altar.

It was not long after he met Denise that he brought her here to show off the town's treasure. His girlfriend is not a churchgoer. But surely a person of her background would appreciate the cathedral's grandeur. Anyway, she, like him, is a devotee of classical music. This is where Mendelsohn's *Elijah* was performed twenty something years ago. I was just sixteen when my father brought me to it. My parents had also been present when Elgar's *Dream of Gerontius* had its Irish premier, way back in the fifties. But before he could point out the intricacies of the architecture, she had pulled the proverbial rug from under him.

"There's no doubt, Peter, that the building is magnificent, and something the town should be proud of. But, isn't it rather lavish. For the time it was built. In a small, midlands town. Have you ever considered the implications of its construction? You say it was built in the early 1930s and must have cost, in today's terms, say a hundred million. During a period of abject poverty in

Ireland? When the people struggled to put food on the table? There are some who might look upon it as a symbol of the Catholic Church's total indifference to the common man."

I should have anticipated that. No point in replying. What can you expect from an English atheist? Well, maybe that's a bit harsh. She is an intelligent woman, after all. You have to be on your toes when you debate with our Denise. That wouldn't have been the first discussion, or should I say, disagreement, we have had over religion. I suppose I could have said that the cathedral could be regarded as a monument to the sacrifice the people made to show their love of God, even in those harsh times. Too late. No good coming up with a rejoinder after the event.

During the pandemic a homeless old man had set up his bed in the side portico of the cathedral, just to the right of the main door. His cardboard underlay and sleeping bag had been neatly set behind one of the columns, affording him a degree of shelter from the wind. Apparently, he had declined to be housed, claiming that any accommodation with a roof was too claustrophobic. No sign of him this evening. Doubtless he was moved on before the grand opening. Poor unfortunate. They say he was a foreigner.

The bent, masked heads file through the front doors, over the echoing marble, passing the large chalice-shaped holy water font, through the tall, mahogany doors to emerge into the vastness of the interior. He pauses, looks around, and takes a deep breath. Great to be back. The faithful have, as usual, packed the front rows of seats. He is used to estimating the number of massgoers. Today there may be three hundred, perhaps swelling later to four hundred. Small in this titanic space. They say it can accommodate over five thousand. Why so few this evening? Is it another sign of dwindling believers or merely people being careful? They're scared of getting the virus.

The masks camouflage faces, but he recognises familiar acquaintances from their gait, from their clothes, their mannerisms. A tall, humped back and shiny, bald head tell him that is George Gaynor, the bank manager. His long, expensive, tweed coat is followed up the aisle by a soiled, cheap excuse for a down-jacket, hanging raggedly on a short man whose posture suggests he might have just got off a horse. The kind of fellow you'd expect to be in Wellingtons. But here we all are, rich and poor; God has no particular favourites.

He spots a neighbour making her way up the side aisle. Janey! There's Margaret. Should I wait for her after the mass and just show a bit of Christian charity and patience? Should I sympathise with her again? No. Done that already. A month since Paddy passed away. Maybe she wants to sympathise with me. Can't handle that just now. Maybe she doesn't even know. Anyway, I have to get home. Mass should finish at twenty to seven, jump in the car, get home before seven. Wait for Hashim to ring. Is that his name, or is it Hashin? Lord, I hope he rings before half-seven. Told Denise's I'd be at her place for eight. Looking forward to a decent cooked meal. Hope it's fish. Haven't had fish for a week. Don't really feel confident about cooking it myself.

Poor auld Paddy. Had religion on the brain. Well, only in his latter years. Became a right "holy mary". Before that he was known to be a bit of a tearaway: drank a lot; great with the lads; best one for dirty jokes; but at home he was dreadful. Gave Margaret a hard time. And their children. People talked of the beatings he meted out. In the Guards, he was. But got the sack over something nobody talks about. Maybe took a backhander too many. Or maybe gave somebody a brutal hiding. What should I do about Margaret? Ah, forget it. I'll meet her again.

Paddy O'Shea was the next-door neighbour of the Sheridans. He and Margaret had moved into Ballyboe nearly thirty years ago. A big man. You had to be if you wanted to be a Guard. Peter's late father was very wary of him. "Big Mayo lout. Guards think they are like priests," he would say, "they expect respect. Well, he won't get any from me. I know all about him. Joxer Higgins came from the same town as him. Born into a bad family, and carried the badness with him. If he hadn't been a Guard he'd have been a criminal."

But, after Peter's father died, Paddy seemed to feel he had more freedom to call in, say hello, ask if there was anything he could help with. Chatted away to Anne, Peter's mother, who was in the early stages of Alzheimer's and didn't quite remember that her husband couldn't stand the man. And then, as old age gradually crept up on him,

Paddy mellowed, became quieter, gave up the drink, and embraced religion. A born-again Christian.

Only three weeks before he died, he had called on Peter. He looked wild and unkept, his trousers badly creased, his rotund, overflowing belly putting great pressure on the lower button of his shirt (which, of course he couldn't see, poor man), his crop of grey hair uncombed.

"I wanted to tell you," he started, "that I had a spiritual experience last night. God came to me."

He paused for effect, looking deep into Peter's eyes for reaction. When none came, he continued, "yes, God told me to let you know that your poor father, Jim, has just been welcomed into heaven."

The corollary of this was that old Jim had to serve the last few years in purgatory, for his life's misdemeanours, that he had not simply soared straight into the arms of the Lord, so, according to Paddy's séance, he had not been entirely a good person. If Jim only knew! He'd have told Paddy where to get off.

Peter thanked Paddy for his message and then politely enquired how Paddy's health was, knowing full well that Paddy had just recovered from a "cold" that had lasted a month. The "cold" his wife suspected to be the virus, but, of course, Paddy was a virus denier. He had decided not to be vaccinated. God, after all, would protect him, if he needed protecting. Margaret herself was triply vaccinated, and she was not shy of letting it be known that her man should stay in his part of the house and keep well away from her.

"Yeah, I had a bit of a cold, y'know, blocked sinuses and a stuffed nose. But, sure I just went up to the cathedral and got meself a bottle of holy water. I snuffed the holy water up me nose and gargled me throat with it. Sure, within a couple of days the auld cold was gone."

Miraculous!

The "cold" did dissipate, but a few weeks later Paddy had a heart attack. Margaret discovered him unconscious on the kitchen floor. He was taken to hospital where, two days later, he suffered a second heart attack and died. The doctors diagnosed that Paddy's "cold" had been Coronavirus – they had detected the antibodies - and it was the after-effects of this that blocked the arteries to Paddy's heart.

Taking his seat – the same seat he always comes to, for Peter is a creature of habit – he settles back to sweep his eyes around and then upwards. It must be all of thirty metres to the ceiling. Over his forty years of coming here he has always wondered about the structure of the roof: behind the ornate plasterwork that is arranged in a grid pattern, is there a framework of steel and timber, or is it solid concrete?

The mass started and coasted on for over half an hour. Peter tried to pay attention, but at times drifted into muses. Oh! here's Bishop Clohessy. The bishop sweeps up to the pulpit. Thanks everyone for coming. Makes a short speech and sweeps away into the hidden corridors of the complex.

Duty done. Off in his Mercedes to another parish. Father Dunlea takes over and starts his homily. What a boring old man Dunlea is. Same auld predictable shit in homily after homily, God forgive me. It's time he retired. Not that that halfwit Collins would be able to run the parish. I haven't been to confession in nearly a year. But I doubt if the two of them compare notes: did you hear the confession of that fellow, Peter Sheridan? No, did you?; No; since the father died and the mother was carted off to the retirement home he has gone downhill; and now he's cavorting with a sinful woman, an English wan, with a bastard child.

A person needs periods in their lives to think. Places where outsiders, anyone, is not going to prod you in the arm or interfere with your train of thought. You have to be alone. Don't move; don't listen; don't even look; just sit there and ponder. Very often these sessions have profound consequences. You might make decisions, whether to buy another bottle of milk or to radically change your lifestyle. When he goes for a run, which he does regularly, usually early in the mornings, there are too many distractions – traffic, people about, plants and flowers. But Peter has three regular periods when he sinks into thought: at a concert when the music does not inspire him; in the mornings before he opens his eyes and gets up; and in church, when the priest is delivering a boring homily. Another sign, perhaps, of his wavering faith.

Peter is a methodical man. You could compare his mind to the display on his laptop, which is carefully arranged in a linear sequence of folders. The titles of the folders read *personal, pictures, work-in-progress, articles published, current travel, food and wine, music*. Each folder is subdivided into sub-folders. Discipline. Over his adult life this discipline has served him well, he believes, in his adopted profession as a travel writer. Plan the trip, get maps of the cities en route, decide on sights, buildings and features that need to be visited, check out flights and car hire, public transport, hotels, lay all of this out on a large sheet of paper, then, and only then, start booking. And so it is with Peter's mind; he systematically arranges it into folders and sub-folders. He tries to avoid randomness. Dismiss loose reflections. Here he is in church about to embark on a period of thought. But not any old thought that might be floating around in his head; no, he chooses a folder, then a sub-folder, and opens it. The folder he opens is entitled *personal*, the sub-folder *Mary* and the sub-sub-folder *Ethiopia*.

Forget the matter of bringing the bodies home. That decision was made and shared with those who needed to know. Even if it had been feasible, how would you know the corpses were actually those of Mary and Amare? And what state would they be in? No, concentrate solely on the living. Paul, Peter's useless excuse for a younger brother, who never showed any love or kindness to Mary when she was alive, now thinks it immoral to leave the body of their sister in some remote area of blackest Africa. Suddenly he has become human, wanting to hold a proper funeral for their sister, complete with corpse. I should go and talk to him again. I should tell him that bringing the boys back will cost a small fortune, and that his part of the Ballyboe estate will have to go towards it. I have to go and talk to Ma too, but, sure, she's away in the clouds; she won't even know who I am, let alone who her daughter Mary is. Was. All she remembers are things in the distant past.

One of Peter's earliest memories was that Sunday, what is it, twenty-nine years ago, here in this cathedral, the day little Mary was Christened. He himself, as a little boy, had insisted that he be Mary's godfather. And she was such a beautiful little baby. Holding her in his arms he felt so proud. The big brother. Peter takes out a clean handkerchief – he always carries a clean handkerchief in his pocket – and, after surreptitiously checking that no one to his left or right is watching him, he wipes salty tears from his eyes. And she had grown to be such a beautiful young woman. How on earth could anyone, even a deranged Tigrayan soldier, ever think of killing her?

Peter's thoughts are interrupted by some commotion around him. People are shifting in their seats. What is it? It's that strange smell that is bothering them. Pungent. Where is it coming from? He looks about him, noticing a smile on the faces of those near him, and then he spots him. The homeless man is here. Inside the cathedral. Is he praying or has he just come in from the cold? He is sitting in the row immediately behind Peter, his skull cap still on his head, his oversized, ragged coat doubly wrapped around him, partially concealing his long, grey beard.

What was that? Dunlea just said something. Was it about the homeless man? No, it was about the bishop and the virus. Missed that. Pity. Was it that he was confirming that the bishop had decided to override the government on allowing people to pray together? Now Dunlea is talking about the Russians getting ready to invade Ukraine. What is the man doing? It's not as if the Ukrainians were good Catholics and the aggressors heathens. Politics and religion have always been kept apart, especially in homilies. Isn't it great for the priest at Mass. He can stand up there and say what he likes, talk utter shite (as Tom Draper would suggest), and nobody can interrupt him, or offer a differing opinion, no censorship. Now Dunlea is asking us to welcome the Ukrainian refugees.

The homeless man shifts in his seat, making himself more comfortable, his eyes closed. Some say we should get our own homeless people housed first, before we start taking in Ukrainians.

As Dunlea issued the words *the mass is ended*....Peter hears a soft purr. He looks around and the homeless man has eased into sleep, a gentle snore emanating from him. He is at peace. There's a lot to be said for having nothing in the world and being at peace with yourself, being able to doze off in the midst of a crowd of people, all of whom have some degree of troubles.

Denise

She peels the potatoes mechanically. One by one. Her mind is elsewhere, far away from potatoes. The din from next door distracts her, but she tries to assemble her thoughts; whether her dinner will be a success; her daughter upstairs, will she behave; what music to play. But the underlining thoughts, the ones that really, really matter, are concerning where their relationship is going. If it is going anywhere.

I know, deep down, that he doesn't like fish. But he will never just come out and say it. God, he's such a frustrating man. Dammit, if you don't like it, say it. Give me some sort of hint. But no. He will be his usual polite self. Very tasty, lovely meal. Irish men can be just too polite. *Sorry, sorry*, the commonest words. Is it due to their history? Dominated by the English. At least he'll like the potatoes. They are roosters, very floury. And the wine. Well, the dinner is built around the wine. Chose the wine, then decide what to eat with it. Well, that's Peter's approach. Jerome says it is one of the best Godellos he has ever tasted. And this is the first importation of it into Ireland. Yes, Godello is one of Peter's preferred grapes. And to set the tone of the evening I'll put on something he likes, em… let me see. Mozart, or Beethoven. Must look through the CDs. Perhaps Tchaikovsky, one of his favourites.

Back to the potatoes. *When all the others were away at Mass I was all hers as we peeled potatoes. They broke the silence, let fall one by one…..* Seamus Heaney's poem momentarily enters her head. Never heard of Seamus Heaney until he told me about him. Very Irish. But I got to love his stuff.

Potatoes! What is it with the Irish and their potatoes? Spuds is what they call them here. Where I come from a potato is a potato. On Sundays we would have them roasted, with the beef and Yorkshire pudding. And, generally, on the other days, when we were having potatoes, we would mash them with a little milk. Not the Irish. No. Milk! Goodness gracious, no. Here they take potatoes seriously. One woman will rave about British Queens, another about Golden Wonders, or Kerr Pinks. But the essential trait of any spud is that, when boiled, they soften around the perimeter. Almost approaching mushy. But only on the outside The Irish say the potato has to be *floury*. Balls of flour is the expression. Some cook the potatoes in their jackets, and when they are boiled, the skin should crack open to reveal a soft inside. I was in Supervalu once. There must have been six different brands of potatoes. I approached the shop assistant who seemed to be in charge of vegetables and asked her which of the brands had the flouriest potato. She looked at me blankly. Then she bade me follow her. Reaching the *home baking* section she pointed to the bags of flour. No, I said, laughing. Before I could explain she said sorry and she was off again. This time it was to the top of the shop where there were bunches of flowers. She was Polish, and she had never heard the expression *floury potato*.

Audrey is singing to herself, the muffled hum of the child coming to her from the top of the stairs. She will have her dolls lined up on the bed, fantasising about which of them the bad witch wants to cast a spell on. She has warned the child, made her sit and listen, very important, after the dinner when I take you to bed, you are to stay there. Stay there all night, and into the morning. Do not, under any circumstances, come to my room. Not until I come and get you. Do you hear me? But why, Mammy? What if I have a bad dream? Then you call me, and I will come to you. It's not fair, Mammy. Is it because of Peter? Does he not want me to see him in the bed?

You can't possibly explain to a seven-year-old that the man who comes to visit (rarely, I might add) can't perform, can't get it up, if there is the threat of a little girl suddenly interrupting proceedings. If there is the possibility of the patter of little feet in the corridor the man just won't even try.

Peter and I usually go out on a Saturday and Audrey stays with her nan. But now the Covid has struck, and Nan has to be isolated. And little children are the most common carriers. Anyway, most restaurants are closed. It is winter, and eating outside is not an option. So, it was either Peter's house or mine. That would mean shifting all of Audrey's stuff – dolls, books, bedclothes, toothbrush, and goodness knows what else. So, dinner is going to be here tonight.

What a contrast. His house so big and spacious, in a wooded, country area; my house terraced, small and pokey, with neighbours front, back and sides. The child loves to visit Ballyboe, to wander in the trees, to play with the dog, safe from traffic. She can just walk out the door and be gone for hours. Not like here where, outside, she has to be watched all the time.

There's that fellow next door. Mossie. If only the walls between us were thicker. Another game on the television. Why does he have to have it so loud? Is he half deaf? He watches Gaelic games, soccer, rugby, even American football. Nine times out of ten when he turns the telly on you hear crowds cheering, the commentator gets excited, he is heading for a crescendo, some fellow has the ball, passes to another, who dribbles it, he's en route towards the goal, and shoots…… then the usual flop. He didn't score. Again! When he's not there and May is on her own she is nearly as bad. Reality rubbish. Love Island, Dancing with the Stars. How can people watch this stuff? She asked me the other day – I was hanging out the wash – was I watching the latest version of Love Island. I think she went away thinking to herself *that English bitch. Looking down her nose at everyone. I asked her if she was watching Love Island, and she virtually told me that sort of programme was for people with only half a brain.*

If only Peter would warm to the child, talk to her, play with her. But, in two years, the two have never gelled.

Peter suggests that the girl is too much attached to her mother, that perhaps the child resents him stealing any of her love. But Peter is not a child person. He just can't sink down to the level of a child, to listen and play their little games, to indulge their fantasies. Then there are all the restrictions he places on her: no, you can't play with that, it is too precious; flush the toilet after you use it; no sharp things on the coffee table in case you scratch it. It seems he set out in the world to be fatherless. Never married. Content with his own, regulated life. No surprises. Daily routines. What can I do? Am I wasting my time trying to change him? How can I get the two of them to crystalise? That would be the biggest hurdle over. Then, surely, we could think about a lasting relationship.

She wonders, hopes, that one day she will experience the same degree of passion that she used to have with Johnny. Peter is nice. Perhaps too nice. He is gentle; he never uses bad language; he is generous; he is educated; you can have an intelligent conversation with him. Like me, he loves classical music. But he's so bloody predictable. Maybe it's me, maybe I should embrace his predictability, live with it, indeed welcome it. Johnny was flamboyant, the life and soul of the party; the celebrity; everyone's friend. It was a pity he was unreliable, and that he felt he needed to distribute his love to every good-looking female he crossed paths with. And now his unreliability is most manifest in that he seldom feels the need to see his daughter. Audrey seems to have given up asking when is Daddy coming. Their only connection to

Johnny's family now is Nan. Nan McMahon, just a wonderful human being. I must ring her, see if she's alright. Maybe Audrey and I could go around to her, if only to stand outside and say hello.

A woman like me can't afford to make two mistakes at this period in her life. Besides, my body, and my head, are telling me that I should have another baby. And, if I am going to have one, then it has to be soon. I only have a few child-bearing years left. It doesn't seem very likely that I could have one with Peter. Well, not as things stand in our relationship. So, Denise, darling, you need to mould this man into the partner, or husband, you want, or accept his shortcomings and carve out a lasting relationship with him. The alternative is to pack it in, give up, and start looking again. And that would entail forgetting about a brother or sister for Audrey. Not easy for a single parent female in her late thirties. Pack in all in, pull up the roots that were sown in Ireland and move back to England. Back to Brexit England. But it would be such a pity to lose Nan. It's nice that a child has at least one grandparent. And Ireland is so much friendlier and homelier than England.

How complex and unpredictable our lives become. We set off on a path, heading in a particular direction, our minds focussed on the goal at the end of the path. Along the way we come to a junction; we know that our direction is straight on, but we decide to make a slight detour, to see where the path to the left takes us; we can always return to the main path; the path to the left seems a good one; so we decide to stay on it; but then we come to a T-junction; here it is not a case of testing one against the other; we have to make a definitive choice, left or right.

I studied history, politics and economics at Birmingham University. A card-carrying member of the Labour Party, destined to enter politics. Put the country right. Get the Tories out. I had a social conscience. The path was clear. Johnny beckoned me to come with him on the left-hand path, and I decided to *suck it and see*. It worked for a while. I can't say that I regret any of it. The T-junction was when I left him. Now I'm on a new path. The goal of a political career is long gone – dead and buried. The new goal is very simple and straightforward; the pursuit of happiness. Not just for me, but for Audrey as well.

Yes, it's nearly two years since I first went on a date with Peter, but the two years have been so disjointed. First of all he was away for several months in South America. Then the Covid broke, and we were all isolated in our homes. You could count the number of times we've been together with your fingers. It's only recently that things have begun to settle. And shortly it looks like he will be off to Ethiopia, for goodness knows how long. Yeah, give the relationship a bit more time. Stable time.

Her mobile rings. Peter.

"Hi. Sorry, but I'm going to be late."

Damn. "Oh?"

"I have to wait for this guy in Ethiopia to ring me back. He's a cousin of Amare's. He's the one who is negotiating for the boys to be released. Land line only."

Amare. Mary's dead husband. Dead Mary's dead husband. Amare, means good-looking in Ethiopian language. That's what Peter told me. But, by all accounts, he was terribly good-looking, for sure. I saw pictures of him.

"So, what time do you reckon?"

"Don't know. Could be half an hour, maybe an hour. I'll send you a text when I'm about to leave."

Turn off the potatoes. "That's no problem, love. I can feed Audrey and put her to bed." Meaning you won't have to put up with a silly child when you arrive, and we can have the evening to ourselves. Haven't decided on the music yet. Did I say Tchaikovsky? No, a bit too obvious. He'll know I put it on just for him. I know, Haydn. One of his quartets. The one that has the German national anthem in it.

His nephews. Now, there's an interesting thought. These two nephews of Peter, suddenly orphaned, needing a home. Who is going to care for them? Not their grandmother, Anne, who's gone cuckoo, and certainly not that good-for-nothing brother of Peter's, Paul, who is more often drunk than sober, who can't cope with his own three children, who can't cope, let's face it, with that wife of his who never cooked the children a decent meal since they were born. At least that's what Peter says. When you think about it, there seems to be only one option – Peter.

Perhaps after a few glasses of wine have loosened his tongue the matter could be explored. Find out what the man is thinking, if, indeed, he has given any degree of thought to it. Hive them both off to a boarding school, perhaps? But he wouldn't be that indurate, would he?

Audrey appears.

"Did you eat everything?"

The child's hesitant nod suggests she didn't.

"Are we going to read more of that story we started, or have you a different story you want me to read?"

"No, I think I'd like the other story again about the purple gorilla."

"But that's a bit scary for you going to bed."

"Ah no, Mammy, sure the gorilla was never going to harm the boy. He only wanted to play."

"O.K. well, you go and clean your teeth. Then put on your pyjamas. I'll come up in a minute."

"Mammy!"

"Yes, pet."

"Could we have a chat afterwards?"

"Off course. Now you go and wash your hands. The dinner will be on the table shortly."

The chat has now been added to the night-time ritual. Teeth, pyjamas, arrange the dolls, story, chat, cuddle, kiss, goodnight.

Anne

Now, where did I put my glasses? Bathroom. No. Did I leave them out beside the television? Feck it, I'll go there in a minute. What was the other thing I was going to do? Clean my teeth, or did I do that already? No, it definitely wasn't that. Ah, I'll just look out the window for a while. Maybe it'll come to me.

Her room is adorned with framed photographs – on the walls, on the window sill and hanging over her bed. The most familiar of these pictures is the one sitting on her window sill. This is the one that she sees, and relates to, most. It shows a middle-aged woman, herself, and a handsome man, whom she vaguely thinks to be Jim, and herself, with three children and a dog. All of the people are in swimming suits, sitting under an umbrella on the beach. It's a happy picture; the colours are bright and gay; the group are all smiling, laughing, in fact. The biggest of the two boys is holding the head of the dog. He probably wants the dog to look at the camera. The smaller boy has a big ball in his hand. She is holding the arms of the toddler, so the baby can stand on the towel. Anne likes the picture because it's happy. Sometimes she waves at the people in it. Hello, great to see you all again. What a lovely day. Was the water very cold? Anne has stopped trying to identify all of the people in the picture. They're her friends, that's all.

The Mount Joseph Retirement Village is a modern, architect-designed, complex that sprawls over a hill deep in the countryside, west of Mullingar. The "village" has a group of ten houses off to one side of the main building. The concept is that when people decide to retire here, they sell their own house, hand the money over to Mount Joseph, and the centre looks after them for the rest of their lives. Initially the ambulant ones go into the houses, where they can be self-sufficient. As they age and become more infirm they are moved into the main building, where they occupy a bedroom.

All of the bedrooms in the main building are arranged around the perimeter, so that they each has a view to open land, to trees, tilled fields, cows and sheep. From her bedroom Anne can look down, over manicured lawns, at the cars and vans that come and go through the main gate. The residents (they are never referred to as *patients,* or anything that might suggest they were here involuntarily) have no external doors they can go through. They can access the central, landscaped yard, around which all of the bedrooms are arranged; they can go into the church, or the dining hall, but approaching a fire-escape door sets off an alarm, when an orderly, or nurse, or matron, will suddenly appear.

The retirement village replaced a former nursing home run for decades by the Little Sisters of Saint Joseph. Whilst the Little Sisters retain the overall ownership of the centre, the day-to-day running of the village is managed by a professional care team. The architect for the village was John Clohessy, whose workload increased enormously when his uncle was appointed Bishop. Every new commission for works related to the Church, or to religious orders, suddenly came John's way.

Those who now live and work in Mount Joseph would be oblivious of the trouble the architect had with the Westmeath Fire Department. The fire officer wanted all of the bedroom doors to be *fire doors*. Now a fire door has to meet certain requirements: it has to be made to withstand a fire on one side – hence, the door becomes quite heavy; it has to have three hinges, fit tightly into the frame, and vision panels have to be small – none of these were onerous issues; but the biggest problem for the architect was the final one – the door has to have a door closer. Older people just can't handle door closers. Nurses find it impossible to negotiate a door closer bringing in trays of food. After months of toing and froing the facility received its fire certificate, complete with fire doors, but without any door closers. All it took was a phone call from the Bishop to the County Manager.

The landscaped inner courtyard is specifically designed to cater for people with dementia. A covered pathway follows around the space, regular in shape, handrails both sides, with features along the way, features that are intended to become landmarks for the afflicted ones. There's a spotted mushroom with a leprechaun sitting on it; further along there a life-sized cow; a doll's house; a dancing girl.

Mount Joseph is not a *nursing home*. At least it is never referred to as such. By the staff. No, it is a retirement village. The word *home* had unacceptable connotations, particularly in Midlands Ireland. *Home* referred to a place where the poor and destitute ended up, being cared for at the expense of the state. The *County Home* in Mullingar was a long stone building attached to the County Hospital. The unfortunates who ended up there were accommodated in large dormitories, with just a metre between beds, the men in one ward, the women in another. It was a dark and dismal place, with the smell of urine hanging over ever space. *Oh, I hope I don't end up in the Home*, would have been the earnest wish of those in their latter years.

She hears a knock on the door, and staff-nurse Radley comes in. Anne can't remember her name, but knows from her uniform that she's one of those people who keep coming and going, people whom she has got used to. She also knows that this little, round nurse is the one who helps her wash, and then combs her hair. Radley takes her every morning to meet big John. John takes her for her stroll around the courtyard. Her favourite landmark is the mushroom with the leprechaun.

"Now, Anne, your son has arrived to see you."

Son? Do I have a son? Oh, yeah. His name is Jim. Have I more than one?

"Which one of them?"

"Peter, the eldest one."

Peter? Did she say Peter? Not Jim?

"Now, Anne, do you want to talk to him here in your room, or maybe you'd like to see him in the visitor's lounge?"

So many questions. Do I have to answer? Pretend I didn't hear.

"Have you seen my glasses anywhere?"

"They're hanging around your neck, love. Will I bring Peter to your room, then? Mind you, I told him that he will have to wear a mask all of the time he is here."

Mask? I hate them. You can't breathe with those darn things over your nose and mouth. Now, where did she say those blessed glasses are? Anne begins to scour the room again for her glasses, not noticing that staff-nurse Radley has left. She's gone! Well, I never. The least she could have done before she disappeared was to find my glasses. She sits and mechanically turns on the television. Daithí and Maura are discussing a dinner recipe with some elderly woman. Anne can just about make out their images. If only I had my glasses.

Presently a tall young man wearing a down-jacket comes into the room. He has a mask on, so she can only see his eyes, but he looks familiar. She thinks he might be Jim, her husband of forty-three years.

"Hello, Ma, how are you today?" the nice young man says. When he takes off his jacket she sees he is wearing a red jumper and blue jeans. A slim, handsome and well-dressed young man. Just as he's always been. But why is he calling me Ma?

"I'm fine. And how are you?"

"Would you mind if I turned off the telly?" he says, reaching over for the remote control.

"Have you seen my glasses anywhere?"

The nice young man (Jim) comes to her and takes the glasses from around her neck to put them on her. "There you are, now."

Anne is somewhat flustered that she didn't realise her glasses were all the time around her neck. Who turned off the telly? I was watching that.

"I brought you a box of your favourite chocolate balls," the nice young man (Jim) says.

"Oh, that was very thoughtful of you. Thanks. They're my favourite."

"Ma, do you remember who I am?"

"Of course I remember who you are." I ought to, we've been married to each other all our lives.

"That's great, Ma."

"Why do you keep calling me Ma?"

"Oh, dear," the nice young man says, then pulls down his mask to under his chin. "It's me, Ma, Peter, your son. Now do you remember?"

"Of course I remember." But I thought you were Jim.

"You have three children, Ma. See them here in the picture. He points to the picture of Anne's "friends" on the window sill. I am the eldest. My name is Peter. Then the second eldest is Paul. And the baby is….was Mary."

"Why are you saying was? Where's Mary now?"

"Ma, Mary is dead. She was killed. In the war in Ethiopia."

Shocked, Anne lifts her hand to cover her mouth. Tears come to her eyes. "Mary. Dead. Killed, you say. Where was that place she was killed in?"

"Ethiopia. It's in Africa. There's been a war there."

"What possessed her to go to Ethiopia? Could she not have stayed at home?"

"She went there with her husband, Amare, and their two children, Omer and Tenen. Amare is Ethiopian."

"Them is very quare names. Say them again."

"Amare, Omer and Tenen. Omer is seven and Tenen is five. They're your grandchildren."

Anne is confused. All these strange names. Grandchildren. Africa. She'd rather just sit and watch the telly. The telly never confuses her: nobody on it asks her questions; she doesn't have to tax her brain watching it; if she gets fed up looking at one station she can flick to another; you can have people chatting, or you can have a Western, or you can watch one car chasing another; what she likes best are those sports shows with big, brawny men crashing into each other trying to hold on to that egg-shaped ball. Rugby, that's it.

"Did you watch the rugby?"

The nice young man smiles to himself, but Anne can't see the smile. He answers, "no, Ma, I didn't watch the rugby. Did you?"

"I did, and it was very exciting. The lads in green were well able for those others in red."

The nice young man who brought the chocolates stands up. God, he is so tall. Just like he's always been.

"Now, Ma, I have to go away for a while."

"Oh, where are you going?"

"I'm going to Ethiopia, to bring back….."

"Ethiopia? Where on earth is that?"

"It's in Africa, Ma. I'm going there to bring Mary's children back."

When Anne gets confused she has two means of escape, depending on her mood and her medication: if she is spirited she becomes frustrated and angry; if she is weary she simply clams up and fails to respond, crawling into her inner self, shutting the door on the world. On this occasion she opts for the latter.

"I'm tired," she says, "it must be time for my nap." And with that she begins to take off her nightdress and pull the bed covers back. As she settles her head onto her pillow she's aware of the nice young man putting on his down-jacket. She sees him approaching her and she is a little taken aback when he kisses her on the forehead.

"I'll see you in about two weeks," he says, "Paul will be coming up to see you while I am away."

Anne doesn't bother to try to figure out why the nice young man is going, where he is going, or who is this fellow Paul. She closes her eyes and sinks into sleep.

Paul

He disengages the clutch and allows the car to glide down off the road, through the gate and into the drive, crunching the stones of the gravel before it brakes in front of the house gate. Home. But big brother is not here. Well, at least Stella is, and the collie comes barking excitedly to greet him. Dogs don't discriminate. Nor does it matter to them how well you are dressed, whether you shaved, or what kind of car you drive. They just remember who fed them, who petted them, who played with them. It's been a long time. Since he was here last. Much longer since he lived here.

He looks around him. In fairness, he is keeping the place well. Paul walks around the drive, the gravel devoid of leaves, weeds and moss, a task their father was so diligent about and Peter has obviously now embraced. The shrubs have been pruned, the daffodils already in full bloom, and the camelias are beginning to shed their delicate petals. Yeah, he's looking after the place as if it was his. Well, it isn't. There are just the two of us now, and I want my share. He takes out a cigarette and sits down on the seat by the gate to wait for his brother. Can't go in. No key. I should have a key. Fuck's sake, the house is half mine. He'll probably install that English floozy here with her stupid-looking daughter, and who knows what'll happen then. I want my cut of the estate. Now. Then he can do what he likes with it. Look at the fuckin car I have. Bloody wreck. I need a new one.

He looks forlornly at the big Volvo. I've had it for ten years. Two hundred and fifty on the clock. Burns as much fuckin oil as it does diesel. If I sought a discount for it as a trade-in, they'd laugh me out of the place.

I badly need a slash. I'll go over here and water something. He looks about him before opening his fork. The steam rises in the chilly air as his urine is directed into a rose bush. Fuck him and his plants. Don't care if I kill this one. In any case, they are half mine. So I can piss where I want. Paul doesn't know the bush is a polyantha rose, nor does he care, and he is oblivious that the nitrogen, potassium and other chemicals in his urine are actually beneficial to the plant.

Paul wanders around the house, sifting as he does through old memories. Memories of childhood, running around the garden, hiding in the bushes, playing with the dog. To him it was a happy childhood. Except for those times when he got into trouble. Big brother was always protecting little sister. I was the bad boy. Why wasn't the old man as strict with Peter as he was with me? Just my fuckin luck not to be the firstborn.

He had some great friends as a child. There was Johnny Dwyer, and Boxer Foran, and there was Paddy Higgins – we called him Hurricane, after the snooker player – and Liam White, the scrawny fellow who was always being picked on. People knew us as the Ballyboe gang. We stuck together and looked out for each other. As country boys you had to in the town. Because there was the big gang from Springfield and another from Patrick Street. Those fuckers would kick the shit out of you. Johnny and I were the leaders of our gang, with Boxer the brawn. Boxer did what he was told, never questioning anything. Of course, he was as stupid as they come. I doubt if he ever passed an exam. But nobody dared to face up to him. He didn't know his own strength. Why, we had to stop him choking the Rank Muldarry from Springfield one day. Had him on the ground squeezing the life out of him. Just 'cause I told him to sort the Rank out. Wonder where he is now? They say he went off to London. Working on the buildings.

The five of us went through primary school together, then secondary school – although poor old Boxer had to go to the Tech, just didn't have it upstairs to survive Latin and stuff. But we were all together in the evenings. Up there on the ditch. We'd sit there talking and doing things we were not supposed to do. It started with smoking, then we got into having a few cans. We used to throw the empty cans below the ditch – there were thousands of them. I thought the old man would blow a fuse when he discovered them. But, no, he looked at it as a great thing. I couldn't believe it. He had cut a channel across the entrance, just under the gate, to stop rainwater coming into the drive, and he needed a soakaway. So, he put in a drain down to our pile of empty cans, covered it all with a sheet of some kinda quilt, and the cans acted as the soakaway. One of the few times I did something that he didn't whinge about. I'd say I was about eighteen then.

It was on my twenty-first birthday, can you imagine, right on the day when you're supposed to get the key of the door, when he gave me the boot. Drinking was one thing, drugs were an entirely different matter. No discussion. He just fucked me out. Said that this was the last straw. Fuck it, we were only smoking the odd joint. Silly auld bollix. Cannabis will be legal here soon.

The house is a traditional stone-built two-storey structure with a slated roof. At the rear it steps down into the garden to provide a small basement. You can detect straight away that I'm not just a yob. No, I'm an engineer. See.

But it was always a cold house. From September through to the following May he remembers the thick sweaters he always wore. Ma knitted them. If you went down to the basement where the washing machine was, and which never gets any sun, it was always bloody freezing. But then the old man and Peter set about insulating the outside walls. And they replaced the windows with double-glazing. I never got the benefit of that. Ma said it transformed the house. But I was gone when they started. Gone? I was booted out. Shown the door. Ballyboe has been in the Sheridan family for donkey's years. The old man wanted it to stay that way. Said so in his will. Well, that will is dead and buried with the auld bollix now. Life moves on.

He hears hammering down the lane. Must be Draper. The queer. If he's still alive. My gang used to torment him. We called him names, making gestures at him. Yeah, but he was very odd. And you couldn't trust a queer. But the old man always had time for him. Could never understand why. And big brother was his best friend. I'd say old Draper was shagging our Peter for years. The old man must of known. Why didn't he do something about it?

Where the fuck is he? His watch tells him that big brother is ten minutes late. Not like him. This is like a summons. You come out to the house, I want to talk to you. What about? About Ma, and about Mary's two children. What've they got to do with me? Yeah, well, I'll listen, and then he's going to get a mouthful of my needs.

Paul is about to take out his mobile when Stella alerts him. Big brother is on his way. How can the dog detect that an electric car is coming? The nearly new, almost silent, little Nissan settles beside Paul's old Volvo estate, the latter nearly double the length of the former.

Better start off cordially. "You're keeping the place well," he greets his brother.

"Ah, nothing else to do during this bloody pandemic. How are you?"

"Grand."

"Sheila and the kids?"

"Yeah, they're all fine."

"All fully recovered?"

"Yeah, not a bother."

Paul's youngest, Shane, brought the virus into the house and, within a few days, they all had it. Nobody was allowed to leave the house. So, it was Peter who had to go shopping for them every day, leaving the bags inside their gate. Bastard wouldn't buy us a few beers. Can you imagine? What's the harm in a few beers? He even baulked at buying us fags. Said we should take the opportunity of giving them up. We asked for burgers, chips, steaks and sliced loaves – white. What did he bring? Minced meat, fuckin minced meat, salad, tomatoes, dirty potatoes, brown soda bread that the kids refused to eat, that turned into concrete after a day, fuckin cabbage and a hunk of bacon. Sheila looked at the bacon. What the fuck do ya do with that? It's all very well him trying to reform us, but, fuck it, we were hungry. By Jesus, when our confinement was up, we fairly made amends. We sure did. Even sneaked out before the ten days were up.

"C'mon into the house. We'll talk there."

He's inviting me into *his* house. Not *our* house.

Paul lights up another cigarette.

Peter stops short of the front door. "Okay, we'll talk here in the porch." Fuck. Still can't smoke in the house. Well, not putting this out. Only just lit it.

"The day after tomorrow I'm off to Ethiopia. To collect Omer and Tenen, and bring them home. I need you to watch out for Ma."

"I do. I was there two weeks ago."

"I mean every other day, Paul, not once a month."

"What's the fuckin point?" Paul raises his voice to a pitch. "She doesn't know who I am?"

"She's your mother."

"But, she's lulu. I could be anyone. Waste of time."

"Lookit, I will be in Ethiopia, with a lot on my plate. I need the peace of mind that our mother is being looked after."

"But, what can I do that the nurses aren't already doing?"

"Show her a bit of love. I know she won't remember who you are. But we have to just persevere."

"I really don't see the point. You go up there…..into her room…she hasn't a clue who you are….what you are doing there…what's the point?"

"Just do it for me, will ya?"

"Couldn't your friend, Tom, call in to her now and again? He has the time and the patience."

"Because of the Covid visiting in the nursing home is restricted to family. I can't believe I have to cajole you into visiting your mother."

"Oh, alright then. I'll go up whenever I get the chance."

"Thanks. You could text me."

Fine. He'll get a text every day – went to see Ma today. She's fine – who will know any different. So long as she doesn't suddenly die. Or fall into a coma.

"Listen, I'm short of cash. I need to replace the car." There, that'll get the matter going. "Can you and I sort out the estate, so I can get my share?"

Peter looks at him as if he had two heads. Then he makes a distinctive sigh and says, "finish that cigarette and let's go inside." Well, when big brother sighs like that, and then asks you to come in and sit down, you just know nothing is going to be easy. He flicks the butt of the cigarette over into the shrubbery and follows big brother through the hall and into the kitchen. Are we getting a drink? Suppose not. Perhaps a cup of tea? Doubtful. Peter pulls out a chair and sits at the kitchen table.

"Now," he begins, and the *now* is signal number two that there will be two chances of Paul extracting money from his brother – little, and none. "I don't need to remind you of father's will." He always called him *father*, but I always refer to him as *the old man*. Go on. Jim Sheridan decreed in his will that the house should stay in the Sheridan family, and that it should not be sold to pay off any of his heirs. But a solicitor acquaintance had told Paul that could be challenged.

"The old man is dead and his will is buried with him. There's just the two of us now, so let's get the matter sorted."

"The two of us? You mean the five of us?"

"Five?"

"Ma is not yet dead. And there is Omer and Tenen."

"What the fuck have those two got to do with it?"

Peter raises his hand. "Hold on. First of all, father's will clearly stated that the house was to remain in the Sheridan family…"

"But…"

"Wait, and let me finish. Mary retained her surname and her sons have the Sheridan name. So, in line with father's wishes, they are heirs to Ballyboe. Now, father's will stated that, in the event that the house *had* to be sold, that you would get ten per cent of the proceeds, after…. mind you, after, all expenses were paid. That was to reflect that I took out a loan to pay for the refurbishment that we did. A loan, I might add, that I am still paying off. Now, Ma may very well have made a will…."

"Can't we find out if she did make a will?"

"Ma could live for many years yet. Where is the money coming from to pay for her nursing home? Bringing Omer and Tenen back is a huge financial outlay. Those who held them demanded a ransom. A million Ethiopian birr. I think that's about twenty thousand euros! I don't know whether I will have to pay that much, or maybe even more. It will cost me several thousand more to go there and bring them home. Have you even thought about any of this?"

"Yeah, well…."

"And you are asking me to cough up money, money that I don't have, to fund you buying a new car?"

"Yeah, well…"

"Listen to me, Paul. You have a good job. You get paid regularly. Sheila has a job. You should be able to manage your affairs. It's you who should be saying to me *are you alright for money, can I help with anything."*

Implicit in that remark about managing my affairs is that he disapproves of my odd flutter on the horses. But I like betting. I get a kick out of it. When your horse is galloping up to the finish, and two other horses are vying with it for the win, well, your adrenalin is just pumping. And when your horse passes the post first, and you've just won a grand, the joy is just unrestrainable.

Before he drove away from Ballyboe Paul sat quietly in the dilapidated Volvo. Jaysus, you get prepared for an event, you practice what you are going to say, you are resolute in what you will accept, and, bang, you not only end up with sweet fanny adams, but you get a ticking off into the bargain. Fuck it.

Father Patrick Dunlea

Father Patrick is a diminutive, yet stocky man with a midriff that has become steadily portlier in the past few years. In his youth his hair was a sandy red, but, now in his late sixties, the hair is a curly grey, bushy and disobedient.

For many years now he has entertained the goal of being elevated in the church, an ambition that has been dismally unsuccessful. He cannot understand why. After all, his credentials are impeccable: joining the church at the very young age of eighteen; working hard at his secondary education; ordained at twenty-two, one of the youngest priests ever from Kerry; five years in the Missions in Africa; it was he who organised relief for the people stricken by drought in northern Kenya; returning to Ireland after suffering from malaria; personal assistant to the Archbishop of Armagh; a clean record in all of the posts he held; not one insinuation, let alone claim, on him during the decades of clerical abuse; provisional parish priest in Mullingar. But, after arriving in the Midlands' town fifteen years ago, all he had since achieved was to be confirmed as the permanent parish priest. And even that took four years, and had to await the death of the previous holder of the office.

His bishop, if he was asked and if he was candid, might have told him that his tendency to easily lose his temper, and his abrasiveness, were the principal causes of his lack of advancement. He might also have told him that bishops, or even potential bishops, are more attentive to their appearance; they are usually a foot taller than he is; they keep themselves reasonably fit and slim; they comb their hair, and get it cut regularly; they shave properly in the mornings; they ensure that their pants are neatly pressed and not overly long so that they bulge out like sacks on top of their shoes. Dunlea's additional failing, that the bishop is not aware of, but would further disadvantage him, is that the parish priest has no concept of modern communications; he is not the owner of a computer; therefore, he has no email address; he has a mobile phone – because one was given to him, but he never uses it – he has to rely on his subordinate, Father Collins for all his mail, all his contact with the world outside of the parochial house. His bishop might also have advised him to lose the strong Kerry accent. And stop referring to his two African priests as *the blacks*.

Nevertheless, our Father Dunlea will press on, oblivious of his failings. His prime objective is to satisfy and impress his bishop, the Very Reverend Edmund Clohessy.

Dump-didily-ump-bump-bum-bum. is a refrain that swims around in his head. Like a punctuation that he uses to conclude a thought process. Generally it is silent, but occasionally, especially when he feels pleased with himself, it emerges from his lips.

Although Father Dunlea has control of the parochial house, the bishop is never far away, and is a regular visitor, because the cathedral, the fulcrum of the diocese of Meath, is right here in Mullingar, and the diocesan office is just out the Dublin road. The parochial house sits immediately beside the cathedral. It accommodates the four priests of the parish, Father Dunlea, Father Michael Collins (from County Clare), Father Obiojulu Yakubu (Nigerian, commonly known as Father Oby) and Father Runako Ncube who hails from Zimbabwe, and likes people to call him simply Father Robert.

How am I supposed to run a parish with the crew I have? Collins the half-wit, stuttering and dillying over every little thing. Two blacks whom the people of Mullingar are simply afraid of. With the two quarest names you could imagine. I find it difficult myself to understand what either of them are saying. It never ceases to amaze me that the two of them can chatter away to each other, with never a *what's that ya said,* or a *say that again,* and anyone listening would think they were talking some African language, when they're conversing all the time in bloody English!

The only normal person in the house is Mrs Simmonds. Doorkeeper, maid, cook, waitress, she performs the lot. Keeps the four of us fed and happy. She's back with us now after an on-and-off presence for the past two years. The pandemic was just terrible. We had to fend for ourselves. Cook, clean, iron, do the washing up. The lot! You couldn't ask that Collins fellow to boil an egg. The two blacks, well, you should have seen the concoctions them boys came up with. Inedible. Far too much spices. Loads of over-cooked rice, not a spud on the plate. I ended up most days just going to Dunnes and buying four readymade dinners. Either that or call Deliveroo.

"Collins," I would say, "ring Deliveroo. I'll have a roast lamb dinner. Yous can order whatever yous like. Tell them to bring it here for seven."

I like to keep abreast of all that is going on in the parish; births, deaths, who is sick, how many of those Ukrainian refugees we are getting; are any of them Catholic. Maybe we could look forward to a Ukrainian priest in the future. The meetings of the parish council were great for gathering information, but, sure with the pandemic we were all locked up, so no meetings. But we'll have one next week. My best source of information is, of course, Mrs Simmonds. That woman has a special talent for it. She manages to suck stuff out from the most unlikely of places. But, I'm a bit annoyed at her. This morning we sat down over a pot of tea. Says I to her, "any sign of that homeless man?" I had run him out of sleeping in behind the columns around the cathedral, then I had to run him from the alcove near the door of the rectory. I told him to be off with himself, and not to be sleeping anywhere near the cathedral. But, sure, I don't know if he even understands me. Foreigner. They say he's from eastern Europe somewhere.

"The homeless man's name is Sergy," she says, "the poor crater is now sleeping in the bushes fornent the garden shed. I saw him coming outta dare yesterday. He was starving. Starving. So I gave him the rest of the roast chicken you fathers didn't ate last night."

"You what?" I couldn't believe my ears.

"And I gave a few warm blankets."

"Jaysus, woman!"

"Ah, Father, the man was starving. Famished."

"Mrs. Simmonds," I says to her, "feeding him only encourages him to stay. We have to get rid of him. He's dirty and he smells. His grace would have a fit if he knew. Get him to go to the social services. They'll feed and look after him."

Charity is all very well, but there has to be some limit. And I can't see why he has to hang around the cathedral. Aren't there plenty of other doorways and alleys to go to.

We'll have our first serious baptism day on Sunday. People are just queuing up to have their babies baptised. Only emergency baptisms were carried out during the pandemic. Isn't that a great sign. I mean, the country is going to the dogs: atheists coming out of the woodwork; all these gay and lesbian people parading around, with no shame on them; mass numbers are falling; our collections on Sundays are bringing in very little – not even enough to feed us. And here we are, with, what is it, eight new babies to be baptised. I'll let the black fellows handle the baptism.

They can't very well make a mess of that. But, I'll be keeping a close eye on them, don't worry.

We had a good mass last night. First one for a long time. And not a bad attendance. For a Saturday evening. If I do say so myself, I thought I delivered a pretty good homily. I made it topical, y'know, mentioning the pandemic and the poor unfortunates fleeing from Ukraine. Dump-didily-ump-bump-bum-bum.

Omer

My name is Omer. I am seven years old. I don't know when my birthday is, but it should be soon, because I haven't had a birthday for a long time. The last time I had a birthday Mama made a cake with candles on it, and I had two of my friends at my party. Their names were Amlak and Liya. Amlak is a boy and Liya is a girl. They live in our street. My brother too was at my party. My brother's name is Tenen. He is five. His birthday is just before mine, so his birthday must be coming very soon. We used to have a calendar on our wall, and Mama would show us when our birthdays were. But that was when we lived in the house with Papa, the house with the trees around it.

We didn't have Christmas this year. I like Christmas 'cause we get presents. I had asked Santa for a bicycle. I think Tenen asked for Lego, but I'm not sure. We got no presents at all.

Our house is in Lalibela. Tenen says Lallybelly 'cause he thinks that's funny. He says there is a Lally with a belly. I know what my name means in Amharic – that's the language of Lalibela. Shall I tell you? It means that I will live a long life. So, you see, with my name of Omer, the Tigrayans can't kill me. I also know what Tenen's name means. It means born on a Monday, 'cause Tenen was born on a Monday. But I don't know which Monday.

Amlak is my best friend. Well, he's my best friend in Lalibela. I have another best friend back in Ireland. His name is Tony. But I haven't seen Tony for a long time. He lives near Mama's house in Mullingar. Amlak and I mainly kick football. But we don't have a good ball. We had one, but some other boys stole it. So Mama made us a ball out of clothes and stuff. I used to play a lot of football with Papa. He was teaching me things. How to take a penalty. How to dribble with the ball. Tenen is no good at football. He's too small. He likes to play with Liya. She has dolls. Sometimes Amlak and me play skipping with Tenen and Liya. But Tenen and Liya are not much good at it, 'cause they can't jump high. So, they have to hold the rope. Tenen gets fed up holding the rope.

Papa's mama used to live with us, but she died. She was sick. The house we lived in was her house. Papa says he was born in the room that Tenen and I sleep in. Well, the room we used to sleep in, 'cause we're not there anymore. We are now going to the big city. There we will meet Mama again. We have not seen Mama for a long time. We miss Mama. And Papa. Helina is coming with us. She has a little bag tied around her, inside her clothes. Our passports are in the bag. But it's a secret. Tenen doesn't know about the bag. Helina told me not to tell anybody. She made me raise my right hand and swear that I wouldn't tell anyone. Helina was the maid in our house in Lalibela. She's nice. When she came to us she didn't speak much proper English. I speak proper English. And I help Helina with it. But Helina's English is now very good. Helina has a brother. His name is Anwar. Tenen and I don't like Anwar. He came to our house one day with Helina. Mama said he was never to come in ever again. She said he stole something. I don't know what he stole, and Mama wouldn't tell me.

Papa was teaching the children in Lalibela. And Mama was helping him. He had a school on the main street. All the people here speak different to us. So, Papa and Mama were teaching the children to speak English. The language they speak is Amharic. But Papa says they have other languages in Ethiopia. The bad soldiers who came spoke a different language. I think it was Tigrayan. I only know a few words of Amharic. Shall I say some? Well, the easiest is to say *Selam*. That means hello. But a lot of people instead say *Iwy salami newy*. I remember that 'cause I like salami, especially when it is new. Amlak can't speak any English. Liya also doesn't speak English. So, I was trying to teach them words. And they were teaching me. I would point to the ball and say "ball". Then Amlak would point and say "ball". But he called it a *kwasy*. Isn't that funny? Then one day Liya held up the rope and said "gemedy", so I said "rope".

One day Papa didn't come home. Mama said that he had to go to the war. We could hear the shooting and the bombs in the hills near the town. We were very frightened. At night we had to sleep on the floor under the table. Mama slept with us and cuddled us.

Then one day those bad soldiers came into Lalibela. They had machine-guns. They shouted at people. When Mama shouted back at them they dragged her away. We were crying. She screamed that she wanted to stay with us. But they took her. Tenen peed in his pants. He often pees in his pants now. He also pees in the bed. Papa's sister told us that Mama would be back soon, but she hasn't come back. Helina is one of Papa's cousins. He has so many cousins. Helina is not allowed to be with us at night. Helina says we are going to the big city. Addis, it is called. There we will be with Mama again. And Uncle Peter is coming also to Addis. He's going to take us all back to Ireland.

We have been travelling now for a long time. And we had to stop many times. Soldiers with guns stopped us. Some of them shouted. Helina said they used very bad words. We have had to sleep on the floor every night. In different houses. A big man was travelling with us. He had a funny name. I thought it was Habtamu, but I don't know. I heard some people calling him Tamu. He wasn't a nice man, but he was the boss. He had a beard. And a long stick. Lots of men in Lalibela have long sticks. He was nearly always on the phone. He was shouting all the time. We were in the back of his van. Me and Tenen and Helina. His van was smelly and it had no seats. And he was smoking all the time. The van had to go over really bad roads, and we were bumping up and down on the hard floor. Sometimes I stood up and held onto the side of the van. That way you didn't get a sore bottom. But Tenen was not able to balance standing up.

Once we stopped near a big lake, so Helina took us down to the lake. We threw stones in the water. Tenen loves to throw stones in the water. But he can't throw them as far as I can. I can even throw stones further than Helina. Then we threw sticks and tried to hit the sticks with more stones. Then we heard Habtamu calling us. When we went back he gave out hell to Helina, and he kept asking her something. When she said nothing he hit her with his stick. But she didn't cry.

We were not allowed to bring anything with us. So we have no story books. Tenen was crying 'cause he couldn't sleep. So, I said "shall I read you a story?" And he said yes. But we had no books. So, I told him the story of Whiffy Wilson. Do you know that story? It's about a wolf who wouldn't go to school. I remembered it cause Mama read it to us a lot. And Tenen remembered it too. I said that Whiffy's friend, the little girl, but I couldn't remember her name, and Tenen remembered that her name was Dotty. So, we kinda told the story together. Then the next night we told the story of *Luke Goes to London.* That's about a squirrel who travels to London, looking for his sister. Only Tenen though it was a fox, not a squirrel. But I'm sure it's a squirrel.

The day before yesterday we drove to a place where aeroplanes used to land. We were waiting for someone. I think we were waiting for Hashim. He is Papa's cousin. Another cousin. We never ever met him before. That's what Helina said. But he didn't come. We waited for a long time. Then some soldiers came with guns. They were pointing the guns at us and shouting. Then they told us to go away. We were not allowed to be in that place.

Yesterday we met Hashim in a different place. Hashim is nice. He asked Helina questions about us. But we didn't know what he asked, cause it was in Amharic. After that he handed a bag with money in it to Habtamu. Habtamu told us to sit down while he counted the money. When he finished he shouted at Hashim. Helina told us that Habtamu wanted more money, but Hashim had no more. They were shouting for a long time before Habtamu went away. He wasn't happy about the money. I'm glad Habtamu is gone. I hated him.

Helina and Hashim are taking us tomorrow morning to a hotel to meet Uncle Peter. Uncle Peter is Mama's brother. He's okay. He lives in the big house where Mama and Grandma used to live. We were told we were going to meet Mama, but now nobody is sure. Uncle Peter is going to take us on the aeroplane back to Ireland. Helina says that Mama might be coming with us, or maybe on another aeroplane the next day. Isn't that great? But I wish Mama was coming with us. We are all going to Uncle Peter's house, so we will be able to play with Stella. Stella is the dog. I hope Helina can come with us. I asked her if she was coming, but she didn't say yes. I think she would like to come.

What do you think of our clothes? This is what Ethiopian men and boys wear. They are like the bed sheets we lie on. Back in Lalibela we didn't wear Ethiopian clothes. We wore the clothes we brought from Ireland.

Hashim says that we must wear these clothes so that nobody will ask about us. I don't like these clothes. Neither does Tenen. They are not very warm. And they are dirty. And smelly.

I asked Tenen what food he would like to eat first when we get to Ireland. He said sausages. And when Mama comes home, potato cakes. We both hate the food in Ethiopia, especially the thing they have like a pancake. But Mama and Papa called it *injera*, not pancake or bread. One day we were out in the country and Papa stopped the car. There were these men in a field cutting grass. They had curved knives and they were grabbing the grass and cutting it. Papa picked up a bunch of the grass and asked us, "Y'know what that is?" We hadn't a clue. Mama didn't even know. *Teff*, I think he called it. He said they cut this grass and chop it up, and then they mush it, and boil it, and pour it on a frying pan like a pancake. Yuk, we said. Can't believe Papa used to eat it. Mama hated it the first time she tried it. She said she swore that her children would never have to eat it.

It seems every meal here you get a plate with this injera pancake spread on it, and then they slop these really spicey stews onto it. But the worst thing of all is that you have to eat it with your hands. You have to tear off a piece of this injera and use it as a scoop to pick up the stew. You should see Tenen after he has eaten. He wipes his hands in his shirt all the time, so his shirt gets filthy. They have no tissues in Ethiopia. I think they call the stew *wat*. We thought that was very funny. Tenen and I would say what's a wat? Since Mama was taken away all we have eaten is this horrible wat and injera. So, I am really looking forward to any other kind of food. And also a spoon, and a fork, so we don't have to get our hands dirty. But I like sausages as well. Yeah, and I love Mama's potato cakes. Just before we went to sleep last night you know what Tenen said to me? Chips. Just one word. Chips. And when we woke up this morning I remembered what he said. You know what I said to him? Ice cream. And he said, "yeah, ice cream. Chocolate ice cream".

Peter

In the animal world it is the male of the species who is predestined to take the initiative when it comes to sex. Generally. But this predestination varies from man to man. If men were to be rated according to their sexual drive, with a rating of one being asexual and ten being totally consumed – someone likely to be either incarcerated or removed from society due to their sexual deviancy – Peter Sheridan might be credited with a rating of two. If three men were standing talking, and a stunningly beautiful woman walked past, those rated seven or eight would be overawed, and fantasise about having sex with her; those rated six would admire her beauty and wonder how they might get to know her; Peter would certainly notice her beauty, but would never be dazzled, suggesting that beautiful females were ten a penny.

As a teenager, Peter found boyish conversations about girls rather uninteresting. He was never impressed by those who boasted of their conquests. He was handsome and tall, and therefore attractive to the opposite sex, but Mullingar is a small town, where everyone knows everyone else, and Peter had the reputation of being a rather uninteresting fellow. Girls whom he dated wanted to talk about Bon Jovi and UB40, and none of them had any interest in Beethoven or Mozart. They wanted to be taken to discos and on romantic adventures, not out into the country to look at wildlife. A girl from Valley Cottages in Patrick Street, looking for a boy above her station, once propositioned Peter. When they were having their first snog she pushed her tongue deep into his mouth. Yuk! Finding that rather disgusting and unhygienic, he had pulled himself free. The girl was shocked, and asked what the matter was. Even though he feigned a discomfort in his mouth, he knew that she knew that it was the first time he had experienced a French kiss. And that he didn't like it one bit. Needless to say, that incident was shared by all of the girls from Patrick Street and beyond.

Peter grew up as a model son. He followed the pursuits of his father and mother, saying his prayers, reading books on nature, listening to music, walking in the countryside, helping around the house. Paul, by contrast, was a wild boy, a rebel. He had to be cajoled into behaving.

In the mornings the Sheridans listed to BBC Radio 4. The parents, that is. Paul was always trying to change the station. Ideally to one with pop music. But, al least to an Irish station.

"Too many adverts and interruptions on RTE, too much repetition," his father would say.

After the nine o'clock news, when his father had gone off to work, Anne Sheridan would switch to BBC Radio 3. Classical music. If anyone asked if she heard Ryan Tubridy this morning she would reply, "I prefer to have nice music than to listen to some compere who thinks he's funny, thinks he's a character, and plays ridiculous, pop music." But don't you love *Marty in the Morning* on Lyric FM? No, she didn't. Marty also thought himself funny, and played pop music.

They bought Paul his own radio, complete with a set of earphones, so that the house would not be plagued by the noise he listened to. It was either 98Fm, RTE2 or 102FM he would be tuned into. Peter became accustomed to the BBC, and gradually got to like it.

Spontaneity was never an attribute of our Peter. Quite the opposite. The words that best describe him would be careful, hesitant and cautious. He liked to keep reasonably fit, going for a run regularly, but that did not go as far as competing in anything. Rugby was horrific, a sure way to become injured. Gaelic football was just an organised brawl. Hurling, running around brandishing wooden weapons, was simply asking for trouble.

Paul, on the other hand, turned out to be a good sportsman. He trained hard, but he was fiery and argumentative. He played hurling for The Green Road, earning the reputation of being tough, and at times, brutal. He had the infamous name of being the most sent-off player in the town league. As soon as he emerged onto the pitch every referee was watching him.

I became known in the town, not as Peter Sheridan from Ballyboe, but as Paul Sheridan's elder brother.

In his late teens Peter thought he might like to be a priest. Perhaps he had a vocation. He had floated the notion with his parents. Anne would have been delighted to have a son a priest, but Jim was more circumspect. He wondered what life the priesthood would make for their son. Would it make him happy? He thought not. Without in any way discouraging the boy, he suggested prayer and further discussion. After a month of reading and thinking about it, and without any input from others, Peter announced that he has dropped the notion.

He was an above average student. You couldn't classify him as being brainy, and he never won any scholarships, but he applied himself to his schooling and he was diligent about his homework, so that he would have been in the upper level of his class. He was good at Geography and English, only average at Mathematics and Science. If there had been a subject in the Leaving Certificate for general knowledge, Peter would have achieved an A. As it was, he earned enough points to study either Law or Engineering – not enough for Medicine, Biotechnology or Actuarial Science, subjects that, in any case, he wasn't particularly interested in – so Peter chose Law.

After a year he began to feel that, perhaps, Law was not the career for him. He had decided to reflect on it over the summer. With his parents he went for a holiday to Sardinia. Jim and Anne had complained that there was very little published information about the island, especially in relation to the ancient monuments there. There were dolmens and portal tombs similar to those in Ireland. Upon returning Peter sought to fill that void in tourism, so he composed a treatise on travel in Sardinia.

His parents were impressed and showered him with praise. That gave Peter the idea that he might like to be a journalist, perhaps a foreign correspondent.

So, in his second year in university he switched to English. His thinking was that, if he later decided to abandon journalism then perhaps he might become a writer, or, worst case, he could teach English.

The only journalistic job he could find, after he had completed his degree in English, was a Court Reporter with Courts News Ireland. The post seemed to have the potential to be interesting. He envisaged attendances at murder trials, gangland crime cases and the like. Instead, he was assigned to cover the family law court, spending hour after hour listening to mundane disputes on family break-up, alimonies, inheritances and ownership of lands.

Paul's secondary education was a continual headache for his parents. Academically he had sufficient capacity. If only he would apply himself to study. He struggled through his Inter Cert. If it wasn't for Jim he would never have secured enough points in his Leaving to enter university. But Jim kept the pressure on, either through harassment or promises of reward. No, you're not going out tonight. Get stuck into Irish, your worst subject. If you don't get the points you will be a labourer for the rest of your days. All I ask is for a few months, probably the most important of your life. What a relief it was when the family learned that he had somehow sneaked into the points category for engineering. Out of university, with a second-class degree, there was no place to go but into the Civil

Service. They needed bodies to fill chairs. Out in the private sector he wouldn't have stood a chance. Consulting engineers would be looking for first-class honours.

Peter's second stint was as a junior reporter for a local newspaper in County Louth. For several years he commuted to Drogheda, returning when he could at weekends. It was a fulfilling job and he liked it. But then his father became ill and he came back to Mullingar, to be with his mother during the trying final years of his father's illness. His degree in English managed to secure him a job as a sub-editor with the Westmeath Independent. His job was to read all of the articles submitted by reporters, to correct their grammar and to properly punctuate their English. He prided himself on his command of language, but became known in the office as *Mister Fussy.* You can't start a sentence with the word *also*; it is not right to repeat a word in the same piece, let alone in the same paragraph.

At least once a week I was allowed to write an article of my own. I remember being asked to go to Dublin on the occasion of Westmeath's first win in the GAA Leinster Football Final. My assignment was to write human stories about Westmeath people coming to Croke Park, their thoughts on their county's very first Leinster win. Forget about the game, the scores, and the players, just write something about the feelings people have on this great sporting occasion, their reaction to being in Croke Park for the first time – that's what the editor told me.

Now, as you know, I'm not a sporting person, and I had never before been to Croke Park, so I was writing about my own awe at being in the stadium. I can tell you I found it a bit frightening, seated in such a huge arena, the noise and enthusiasm of the crowd, the frenzy of them when their team had the ball. I was trying to interview a small boy who had come up from Kinnegad, but, sure, every time Westmeath had the ball he was jumping up and down and had little time for me.

At half-time I felt the need to go to the toilet. Have you ever been to the Gents in Croke Park? It is the biggest toilet I have ever been in. You queued to get in; once in, you stood in line; there were three rows of us, waiting for those at the urinal to finish; the urinal was one long, stainless steel trough; each row shuffled forward as the row doing their pee finished; once the person at the urinal in front of you was finished, you moved quickly in; if you were slow you could feel the frustration of those behind you.

When I got to the urinal, I just couldn't do it. I was intimidated. Too much pressure to perform. All those eyes on my back. Nothing would come out. So, I zipped up and moved away, pretending I had finished. When I got outside, well, I still needed a pee, but I wasn't going through that again. I got into a second queue, this time for the toilet cubicles. It was endless. However, once I was able to turn the lock on the door, I was relaxed and able to go.

I had been with the Independent for barely a year when the vacancy arose of Travel Writer with the Irish Times. It was a freelance post, working as a self-employed writer, and free, therefore, to submit articles to other media outlets, excluding, of course, rival newspapers.

Oddly enough, the first article I wrote for the Irish Times was on Sardinia. I spent four weeks there, traveling the length and breadth of the island. My piece was very well received and, shortly afterwards, I was contacted by The Guardian. Whereas other travel writers simply told their readers the good aspects of the place, I also pointed out the bad ones, the pitfalls, the parts that were not worth going to see, or were too crowded. The Guardian wanted me to provide them with a similar essay on the island, asking me to include food and wine in my discourse. There was a little bit of controversy when I wrote that the Cannonau grape of Sardinia was not an exclusive grape to the island, but was, in fact, pure Grenache, brought back to Sardinia after the phylloxera. Heresy! No, Cannonau was the proud grape of Sardinia, quite different to Grenache, the letters to the editor said. But I had done my research. I knew I was right.

With the article in The Guardian my career kicked off. The Cannonau storm brought me also into wine tourism. I could go to a country and write about hotels, resorts and sights to see, but I could also delve into viniculture. Quite suddenly, from being an unknown, I was being sought after, and I soon had to programme myself to satisfy all of the requests that came in. I even thought about hiring a secretary.

As a travel writer Peter was a solitary agent. Being alone in a strange land, for weeks not meeting a familiar face, didn't cost him a thought. He liked it. And when he returned to Mullingar he would spend further weeks at his computer, writing. Consequently, though not consciously, he hardly ever mixed socially in the town, possibly one of the most important explanations as to why he never established any lasting relationships, particularly with a woman.

Ever since he was a teenager Peter liked to keep himself in trim. Not fit, just trim. Enough exercise so that the brain sent a message to the body not to overdue eating, because the heart needed his weight kept under control. When the weather allowed it, he would run – out of the house and into the country, sticking to backroads and boreens, at least five kilometres, but ideally ten kilometres. When the weather was inclement, quite often in Mullingar, he had an exercise bike in the basement. An hour pumping the pedals, building up a sweat.

His favourite time of the day to exercise was first thing in the mornings. Get up, make a cup of tea. Slice of toast. Then off. Come back and start preparing the breakfast. Allow the body to cool down. Then shower, dress, and eat. He loved running in the early mornings when he was abroad. The best way to get to know a city is to run it just as the city is awakening. You find your way around the streets; you build a mental picture of the street layout. In cities such as Nice, Malaga and San Francisco, there are excellent seafront promenades to run; in others, like Rome, Siena and Prague, you can run along the banks of the river. In the early mornings you see features that you wouldn't notice during the day; you become aware of the traders setting up their stalls, the farmers and fishermen delivering their fresh produce, the busy office workers getting a coffee fix. But, there are some cities where running, at any time of the day, is out of the question. Take Kathmandu or New Delhi, for instance, well, the place is teeming with people. Every street is jam-packed. And nobody would dream of going for a run there. Just isn't done. Oh, and add Addis Ababa to that list.

It's ages since I was away, since I had a schedule to fulfil, a notebook in one hand, camera over my shoulder and a map in my pocket. And I feel a yearning for it: the sense of adventure; of discovery; a degree of danger.

Now, let me think about Denise for a while. I met Denise in Jerome's shop. She seemed to know her wines and she was very helpful. But, then one day I went in there and was about to ask her a question about something – can't remember what – when, out of nowhere, she point blank enquired if I was thinking of asking her out. Well, I wasn't. I wasn't thinking of asking her out. The thought never entered my head. How she got that notion I dunno. Maybe it was the way I looked at her. Gave her the idea that I was interested. Anyway, I couldn't very well say that I wasn't thinking of that. It would have been downright cruel. She seemed to be appealing, quite bubbly, and not bad looking, so I thought, what the hell. Might be good company. So, I found myself admitting to have been thinking of asking her out. At the time Ma was beginning to talk gibberish, and it might be nice to have someone intelligent to spend an evening with.

It didn't bother me when she said she was a divorced, single mother. Neither did it cost me a thought that she was English, or that she had no religion. Well, I was used to meeting all sorts. Y'know, you're off in a foreign land. It's probably unlikely that people you meet are of your religion. We had a nice evening, and I was happy to repeat it. Now, here I am in a fairly permanent relationship. I never, for a minute, expected to be going out with someone for, what is it now, must be two years. Women don't tend to stick with me for any length of time. Generally they are gone after the first date, if not, definitely after the second one.

I must include in my prayers tonight the following: fornicating out of wedlock with an atheist; God help me with my faith – I'm in serious danger of losing it; I'll pray that everything goes well in Ethiopia; pray for Ma and her Alzheimer's; for Paul that he will become a better person (Janey I'm praying all my life for that).

Denise

"Have you seen the Westmeath Examiner?"

That was the start of it. The Westmeath Examiner. What a stupid question. I've never bought, or even looked at the Westmeath Examiner. It's just local gossip. Peter's agitated voice on the phone this morning told her that there was an article about the murder of Mary in Ethiopia. Whatever she did, he said, don't talk to any reporters. Why would any reporter be coming near me?

It is late evening. Denise is sitting at her kitchen table. Audrey is safely in bed and this is her time for herself. Have a cup of tea. Sometimes she scans the television channels to see if there is anything on. Most times there isn't. On the table before her tonight is the local newspaper.

It had not been a busy day in the Mullingar Wine Emporium. Thursdays are never busy. People in the midlands of Ireland apparently only drink wine at the weekends. Tomorrow would be busier and on Saturday the shop would be bustling. The only customer of any significance whom she had to deal with was a young woman about to be married. From the outset Denise knew that the girl – false eyelashes and heavily perfumed - hadn't a clue about wine.

"We're getting married in June. That is, if the hotel is able to have the wedding. They don't know yet. It's the pandemic. If we are restricted to only fifty guests then my boyfriend and I think we should postpone it. You can't have a wedding with just fifty guests. But the hotel wants us to book and pay a deposit. Well, we're not doing that until we know for sure."

Better interrupt her before she goes off on another tangent.

"What sort of wines did you have in mind?"

"Well, Packy – that's my boyfriend – he says we want a white and a red. Preferably French. Definitely not Chardonnay. That's what he said."

Another ABC. We get lots of them. Anything but Chardonnay. If you are brazen enough, and you are sure that they are wine philistines you offer them a taste of Chablis. Oh, yes, that's a lovely wine. We'll have that. You are on tenterhooks in case they ask about the grape. But they never do. You can't wait to have a laugh with Jerome. And they want French! The uneducated world thinks that the only country to produce good wines is France.

"And do you have any price range in mind?"

"Well, we want nice wines, Y'know, ones that will impress. But not expensive. We were thinking under ten euros."

Denise's reaction to the ten euro was to suggest that she go to Aldi or Lidl, but then she knew that Jerome would have wanted her to explore every possibility for a sale before giving up. She thought about offering False Eyelashes and Packy a tasting, but threw that out. Not worth it for a few cases of wine. And no guarantee that they would then buy anything. Already resigned to this being a lost cause, Denise went through the motions of taking False Eyelashes through the store.

The Mullingar Wine Emporium is the only dedicated wine shop in the town. Occasionally a wine connoisseur will enter, and they are just a joy to deal with. When Jerome is in the shop, if he suspects that the customer is one of them, he will descend on him/her. Jerome is very proud of his knowledge of wine, and even prouder of his stock, most of which he sourced himself. His specialities are the wines of Italy and Spain, generally the reds, and dessert wines from anywhere in the world. But price is and has always been a secondary matter for Jerome. Hence, many of the wines on his shelves are rather expensive. So, he doesn't cater for the plonk that False Eyelashes is after.

Denise has been suggesting to her boss that the shop might experiment with wine tasting courses, or wine tasting evenings. She has also suggested that they could offer morsels of tasty food to go with the wines. They could advertise; put a notice in the window; insert one in the local paper; staple a flyer with every receipt. Jerome is thinking about it.

It was one such day, was it two years ago, no, not that long, when the tall Mister Peter Sheridan walked into the shop. He had initially enquired of the whereabouts of Jerome, who was off in Spain on one of his trips, and then he had gone off to survey the shelves. Not finding what he was looking for he had returned to the counter.

"You used to have a Monastrell from Alicante, but I don't see any over there?" he enquired.

"Ah, the Juan Gil from Jumilla. We are having a difficulty getting that (don't tell him that the winery is now selling everything that is shipped to Ireland to Dunnes). But we have an excellent Monastrell from the Sierra Norte in Alicante. I'll show you." And with that she came out to take him to view their newly acquired Pasión. "I think you'll find that a worthy replacement, although, in my opinion, it is superior to the Juan Gil." There, that should impress him.

And it did. Especially her correct pronunciations of Juan, Gil and Jumilla. She had hooked him. With her knowledge of wine and her flashing eyelids. Line and sinker. Peter Sheridan, travel writer, single, well-dressed, softly spoken, tall and handsome. A woman can instinctively tell when she has hooked a man. The facial expressions, the smile, the look, the tell-tale signs. When Jerome returned she found out all about this Peter Sheridan. A most important attribute was that he wasn't married. And that he lived on his own in a big house.

Of course, I Googled him. Isn't Google marvellous! Just typed in his name and up came a whole flood of references to him. Articles he wrote about the most exotic places. He must be the most travelled person I ever knew. And I really like the way he writes; clear and well-structured pieces. No wonder he seems to be well got with editors.

It was shortly after she had irrevocably called time on Johnny, and she was wondering if she should go home to Banbury or try to forge an independent life in Mullingar. Before she had even given the matter serious thought Peter was back in the shop. Fumbling and flustering with his words. She knew he was not just back for more wine. The body language was a giveaway. He wanted to ask her something, but he just didn't seem to be able to compose his question. Detecting his problem, she helped him.

"Are you thinking of asking me out?" Barefaced. And with a glint in her eye.

The tall Peter faked a taken-aback expression. His face gradually changed to a smile. "Well, yes, actually I was." And that was it. Peter and Denise became an item.

Back to False Eyelashes.

"I'll go and talk to Packy. You have some nice wines, alright. Maybe he'll come back with me another time."

Yeah, maybe he will. But, she knew that he wouldn't. That would be the last she would see of False Eyelashes.

On this blustery Thursday afternoon Denise had finally found time to pop out to the newsagent and purchase the local paper. The headline on the front page was startling. "One million euro ransom for murdered Mullingar woman's children", it read. No wonder Peter was furious. Did I talk to anyone? No, I certainly did not. Then it must have been that hair-brained brother of his, Paul, he supposed.

"I told him a million birr, not euros."

Mullingar is a small town. A small provincial town. Where your business becomes everyone else's. And, being Irish, everybody wants to know as much as possible about everybody else. It's part of the Irish psyche. Banbury, by contrast is about twice the size of Mullingar, so that knowledge of others is a little less. But the English just are not as nosey as the Irish. You wouldn't dream of gossiping openly about your neighbours. The Irish take pleasure in it. Did you hear about missus so-and-so, well, come 'ere till I tell you a good one. Their nosiness doesn't really bother me, it just makes me laugh.

Nosiness reaches an apogee when there is a juicy story about. And the story that everyone wants to hear about is the ransom for the dead woman's boys. You become a celebrity if you have inside information. No sooner had Denise arrived home when May next door was out looking for her, calling her from over the wall. A woman whom she has rarely spoken to in two years now wants to chat. She wants to pump me for information, that's all.

May is a big woman. All of a hundred and ten kilos. Probably mid to late forties. Her hair is bleach blonde, never appears to be combed, and in need of the bleach being replenished. Her clothes are loose-fit, big knitted jumper over a shirt and flabby pants. As is often the case with women of such posture, she laughs a lot, and when she does her frame flops up and down. Mossie, the husband, is equally big, and so are their children. All the result, to my way of thinking, of eating the wrong food.

And wouldn't you know it, she starts off first with the weather. All conversations in Ireland start with the weather. It's a national obsession. Then she moves to Ukraine. Why doesn't she come right out and ask about the dead woman and the ransom? No, beat about the bush, hope that the other party will bring up the matter. Well, I'm not going to mention it. Talking about this delicate subject with an outsider would not be right.

"So, I see that Peter will soon be off to Ethiopia to bring the boys home. You must give him our regards. Best of luck to him. Them poor children."

There. May couldn't wait any longer. I will say the minimum that is proper.

"Yes, he's off soon."

Not enough for May. She needs more.

"Can we do anything to help? Mossie was saying that people in the town are planning a collection. To help with the ransom."

"Well, as far as I know, there is no ransom." Well, I had to say something. Couldn't just let them start collecting.

"No?" The woman is surprised.

"No, it's just the expense of getting them to the capital and then getting them home."

"So, is the story in the paper all wrong? About the million euro ransom?"

"Now, May, I'm not directly involved, but I do know that the story in the paper is just rubbish."

"Oh. I see."

There is an unwritten rule in Ireland, it seems to me, that information, dare I call it simple gossip, is traded. I have something juicy to tell you, but you must reciprocate. Mossie, I found out, is from Cork. Down there they don't say *gossip*, they say *sca*. Have you any sca, they would say. May is telling me all this, nudging me on to open up to her. She gets some of her sca in first.

So now I know a little more about the Sheridans. Sorry, but I do believe I am falling into the Irish gossip ways, talking like this. Anyway, as they say over here, c'mere 'til I tell you. Jim and Anne Sheridan come from a well-respected family, very staunch Catholics. Always voted Fine Gael. Didn't trust the Fianna Fallers. Jim would turn in his grave if he knew that two of his children were no longer churchgoers, and that one of them, Paul, now supported Sinn Fein. Paul, was always a difficult boy, from the day he was born. Getting into trouble at school. He certainly did not follow in Peter's footsteps. Had to have grinds in secondary school to get him through the Leaving. Then he and his friends began to smoke pot, and the Guards were on to them. The ignominy Jim felt when the Guards came to the house to search for drugs. They found so much in Paul's room that they were on the verge of classifying him as a dealer. He was extremely lucky to get off with a warning. Then, only a month later, Jim found Paul with more drugs, after him warning the lad that this was his last chance, Paul was shown the door.

Peter wouldn't tell me any details like that. Sure he whinges about his brother, but he'll never divulge too much about his family.

Now the next bit May told me was about Peter's neighbour and friend, Tom Draper, whom I've heard about but never met. From what Peter told me, Tom is a nice old man who lives down the lane from him. Apparently, Tom is a horticulturist and also has a keen interest in classical music. Peter and he are often pottering around the garden, and they have been to the odd concert. Well, wait till I tell you what May told me.

The Drapers were farmers who originally owned Ballyboe House and all of the surrounding lands. They had four children, Michael, Paddy, Tom and Josie. The only one of the four to remain was Tom. When the old folks died the estate had to be divided up. The only recourse was to sell the lands, including Ballyboe House. That was when the Sheridans appeared. They bought the house, and Tom moved down the road to a farming cottage.

Well, that all seemed simple, interesting background, but not really juicy. Then May hit her with a sucker punch.

"You do know that Tom Draper is as bent as a stick?"

Denise was not going to let her away with that. She knew exactly what May meant, but she wanted to gather herself for the defence of homosexuals.

"I don't follow you."

"He's bent. Y'know, gay."

"So what. I have a sister who is gay. It's natural. At least ten per cent of the population is gay."

"Well," May began with a heavy sigh, "I don't know about it being natural, but, anyway, Tom was known to be interfering with young boys."

She waited for that to sink and followed up. "The Guards were out to him several times. When a child was interfered with in the town Tom was regularly hauled in."

Not knowing any details, Denise could not defend Tom, and she remained silent. With the bit between her teeth May followed up, "you know that there was talk about your Peter and Tom?"

"What?" Denise could not believe her ears.

"Oh, yeah. Peter was known to spend lots of time in Tom's cottage. Oh, yeah, they were thought to be quite close. So close that Peter was also regarded as being gay. Now, don't get me wrong, you must know more about Peter than I do, but he seems such a nice man…."

Denise was left speechless. Peter had never mentioned that Tom was gay. Could it be that Peter was bisexual, what someone, she couldn't remember who, referred to as ambidextrous? She'd have to get away and think. Think about whether it was possible; would that explain his reticence in bed; if it was, did it matter?

Escape.

"Oh, I think I hear the phone. I'd better go. Talk to you again."

Tom

It is Saturday evening and Tom Draper is getting ready to go out. He always goes out on Saturday evenings. It's the highlight of his week. He makes a special effort for this; his good trousers, sports jacket, what he calls his dancing shoes; he showers, trims his beard, cuts his nails; he uses his electric trimmer to clip off any hairs that protrude – from his nose, out of his ears, around the backs of his ears.

Tom is going to meet his friends.

We jokingly call ourselves the Mullingar LGBT Senior Society, the MLGBs. We MLGBs don't mix with the younger LGBT lot, although they now refer to themselves as the LGBTQI, none of us know what the Q or the I stand for. So, we don't march in the Pride parades, but we like to see them out, telling the world that we exist.

There are only four of us, so *society* might be a little farfetched. The eldest of the four is Kevin. He and Tom have known each other for forty years. Indeed, they have been a couple for virtually all of that time. Kevin is now a feeble old man, in the early stages of Parkinson's, unable to climb stairs, has to be driven everywhere, has a *home help* calling to him twice a day. Tom looks in on him most days, buys his messages, occasionally spends the night. But Kevin still has his faculties about him. He reads a lot, keeps himself abreast of current affairs, and loves to talk politics. Tom and Kevin did consider getting married, when same sex marriage became legal in Ireland, but neither of them then were very enthusiastic about it. Kevin has been an outspoken conservative all his life, a stance that has, on occasions divided Tom and him. Kevin is a retired civil servant, having worked as a planner for Westmeath County Council for forty and more years. In the early years of their relationship Kevin would not venture down the lane at Ballyboe, because he was scared of the boys who sat on the ditch watching and jibing. So, Tom and he shared the house in the town, on a busy street where nobody would be monitoring who came in and who went out.

But living in the town is not for me. I need air. Country air. And peace at night from the traffic. I must've spent years trying to coax Kevin into moving in with me, but he's a townie. I see now that the matter of the boys on the ditch wasn't the main issue. He likes to get up in the morning and go to the shop. Out at Ballyboe he would have to get in the car. Howandever, the Parkinson's may have changed his tune, and I think he's coming around to moving to Ballyboe. I can wait on him hand and foot there.

Georgina is the youngest of the four, and she is the one who organises them. It's your turn this week to bring the booze; we will meet next week in my house; why don't we make a trip to the seaside next Saturday. Doubtless, she will bring antigen test kits with her, so that she can decree whether we wear masks or not. Georgina is Russian.

Rather, Georgina is a refugee from Russia. She was a social worker there.

In her country of birth there is no tolerance for gay or trans people, and Georgina was born Grigory. Although all of her outward appearances are female – she prefers dresses rather than pants; she wears floppy jewellery, long ear-rings; her blouses are always low cut - she retains a croaking masculine voice, and her mannerisms are not what you would expect of a female. She drinks beer in pints, talks and laughs loudly. Georgina is a big girl. Whatever medication she has to continually take for her condition, it makes her bloated. Her political perspective would be to the left of centre, so that she and Kevin regularly hop off each other.

Finally there is Cora, who is lesbian. Cora and Georgina have had an on/off relationship for some years now, and neither Tom nor Kevin know what the current situation is. Tom would guess that Cora is in her late sixties, perhaps five or more years older than Georgina. And Kevin will be ninety next year, nearly twelve years older than Tom. Cora, according to Tom, wavers in her political views. In fact Cora only enters debates, whether it is about politics, or religion, climate change, or any other topical subject, to inject controversy. She is lazy, lounging in her chair, listening, and picking her time to interject. Cora used to be a schoolteacher. She dabbles in poetry, regularly trotting out verses she has composed. Verses that Kevin considers an insult to poetry. But he wouldn't dream of telling anyone, except Tom.

To be fair, I'd better tell you about myself. First of all I am the only one of the four of us who is from the town. The rest are blow-ins. I'm the only one with the courage to come out, and then remain in the community I was born in. The rest of them moved, so that they wouldn't have to proclaim their sexual orientation and then face their kit, kin and schoolmates. Kevin is from Tullamore, or somewhere between it and Portarlington, anyway, another Midlands man; Georgina from St. Petersburg, formerly Leningrad; and Cora hails from Aberdeen. I've hardly ever been anywhere outside of Mullingar, certainly never lived or spent more than a week away from the town. You'll hear, when I talk, my dialect, known as the *Midlands Mumble*. Kevin has it as well. A lot of people would be a *hape of people*; an unfortunate, likeable person would be a *poor crater*; a small boy would be a *gasson* (I think that's from the Irish *gasún)*; a blackguard or a bad person would be referred to as a *cur*, and a person who looks ill would look *shuck* in Mullingar. When I go to Dunnes Stores or Tesco I am going, not for my groceries, but my *messages*. When you ask a Midlands person a question he will often start his reply with *lookit*. Something similar to using the word *so,* or *well*. I'm a whore for black chocolate, meaning, in Mullingar, that I like the stuff and eat a lot of it. Kevin is a wine person. Me, I like a drop of whiskey. Tonight the other two will be drinking beer. Since it's my turn to bring the drink, I have a bag of cans, a bottle of Merlot and a single malt.

I've been a gardener all my life. I don't really read a lot, but I listen to music. I studied for the Leaving Cert, but I never took the exam. You might consider me the least educated of the four. My leaning would be far-left. In an election I would vote Socialist, if one is standing, alternatively Labour, and, using our proportional representation voting system, put Fianna Fail before Fine Gael. I have no truck with People Before Profit, considering them mere anarchists for the sake of being anarchists, or Sinn Fein who masquerade as national socialists. The last great national socialist was Adolf Hitler.

I spent thirty years with the Health Board, initially looking after the grounds of Mullingar General Hospital, but in my final years I was the landscaping supervisor for the Midland Health Region. So, I retired with a dacent pension (meaning a decent retirement income).

You want me to describe my physical appearance? Lookit. Have to start the reply with *lookit.* I've been a healthy man all me life, some people might add, *thank God.* That's despite the fact that I smoke. I'd say I could count the number of times I've been confined to hospital on the fingers of one hand. Sure, at seventy-eight I'm slow and bent over a bit, what do you expect. I'm average height, weigh twelve stone (none of those kilo yokes for me) and I have a tightly trimmed beard. I still have a bit of hair on my head, but it gets thinner everytime I look in the mirror to examine it.

The weather is important to a gardener. It will determine whether he is going to be out in the fresh air or in the greenhouse, whether the grass can be cut today or better put off for a few days. I never fail to listen to the weather forecast every morning and every evening. Inevitably my first topic, when I meet anybody, is to talk about the weather. Some people, particularly foreigners, find that comical. I once met a fella, he was German, who came to Ireland to work as a meteorologist. He said that, if you wanted to be a good driver you should drive a taxi in Berlin; if you wanted to be a good meteorologist you should work for a while in Ireland. The most variable, unpredictable weather, he said, in the world was here in Ireland.

We had one of the wettest Februarys for decades this year, but March is turning out to be very dry. I always say that the amount of rain we get averages itself out, so that if we get a wet month, or season, you can bet that the following one will be dry, and vice versa.

Immediately he entered Georgina's house Tom was handed an antigen test kit. Georgina had somehow acquired a box of these – none of them were to ask where she got it – and they all sat quietly inserting the probe up their noses, squeezing the drops onto the plastic stick, then waiting so see if a second line appeared. Negative. No line. Kevin was not sure.

"Give it to me," Georgina commanded, "ah, you mustn't have put it enough up your nose. Here, we'll start again on a new kit."

The others waited. Twenty minutes later Georgina announced that Kevin was also negative.

"Right, girls, hand them over." She examined the four sticks. "Janey, Tom, you're positive."

They all looked at Tom.

"Deed I'm not," said Tom.

"You are. Look. There's a second line there."

Tom took the stick and peered at it. "Jaysus, it's only a faint line. It just couldn't be that I'm positive. Sure, I've been jabbed two times, and I've no symptoms."

"Vaccinations don't protect you from the virus, they merely ensure that, if you get it, the effect on you will be diminished. Symptoms or not, boy, you're positive," said Georgina, "so back on with your mask. And you sit well away from us. The rest of us can put the masks away." Tom was relegated to the corner of the room for the evening. Before he moved Tom and Kevin exchanged anxious glances at each other. Doubtless they were both reflecting on their various moments of togetherness over the past few days. There were no kisses or intimacies to be worried about, but they had been close, very close.

Now that I think about it, I was a bit chesty during the week, but I thought it might be just the pollen in the air or dust or something. Well, if this is the virus, sure 'tis harmless. Harmless. If I am positive then I'm delighted. Then I won't ever be afraid of the damn thing ever again. But, Jaysus, if I gave it to Kevin, well, what affect would it have on him? Let me think. We touched, a few times, but they say that the virus is not transferred by touch. The damn thing is airborne. I gave Kevin a kiss on the forehead, yes. But I was never, I don't think, up in his face, talking. Was I?

Tom expected the evening's conversation to start off with a cross-examination of him about the two boys and the ransom, but, no, they had to solve world affairs first. Kevin got stuck into Georgina from the outset.

"Your friend, Putin, is not having it his own way in Ukraine, I see," he prodded.

"My friend?" Georgina's voice was vexed. "Are you joking me? Putin is one of the main reasons I'm here in Ireland."

Tom ventured, "hard to know what the outcome will be."

"Well," Georgina began, "I'm predicting that that bastard will be dead within six months. He will wreck the Russian economy, and the oligarchs will have no alternative but to get rid of him. And there's no way he'll go quietly."

They kicked the War in Ukraine around until the subject was exhausted, and then they moved to the US, via Biden to Trump and the possibility of him being indited over the January 6th assault on the capital. Cora's opinion that Trump would be back in 2024 as the next president sent sparks flying. Even Kevin was dismissive of it. All of them agreed that Boris Johnson and Donald Trump were egotists. It was Georgina who put it so succinctly: she suggested that they both craved public adoration, but that the difference between them was that Johnson was a foolish, lying egotist, but Trump was a clever, conniving one.

The debate had subsided; Georgina had put on the kettle for Kevin to make his tea; the others had topped up their drinks. Then Georgina asked the inevitable.

"So, tell us about these two boys and the Ethiopian ransom."

Tom took a sip of his single malt and composed himself.

"There's no ransom. That's a load of rubbish. It's just some fella in Ethiopia making a few bob for bringing the children from the war area to the capital. The uncle of the boys is going out to collect them, I think in a day or two."

Tom left it at that.

"Ah, c'mon now, Tom. Give us a bit more detail." Cora wasn't going to let it lie there.

"There's little more to be said. Them two little gassons will be in Ballyboe in a few days. That's all I know."

"And what then?" Cora pressed. "Who's going to look after them? Will that uncle of theirs be their guardian?"

"I dunno. Suppose so."

Kevin got up and made himself a pot of tea. While it was brewing he went to the toilet. That was when we had a laugh at his expense. You see, our Kevin has a shake in his right hand. Quite a distinctive shake. He says it's not from the Parkinson's, but I'm sure it is. While he was in the toilet didn't Georgina pick up a cup and the teapot. She moved around the room, her hand shaking the teapot with its boiling contents, threatening to spill it over people, and imitating Missus Doyle from *Father Ted*, she was saying "would ya like a cup a tae. Are ya sure? Ah go on, have a cup a tae."

Anne

Anne is not feeling well. She has a pain in her shoulder from the vaccination she received early this morning. But the shoulder pain is quite a minor part of her discomfort. She has developed a fever; her head is throbbing, and her nose is blocked. She thinks it's a cold coming on. Perhaps a flu. She is inclined to lay the blame at the way she was handled leading up to the vaccination and the hanging around after it. There was a cold wind blowing through the corridor whilst she had to sit in a wheelchair. For over an hour. What was she being vaccinated for anyway?

A doctor and nurse had called to the retirement home to administer the vaccinations. Tragically, neither the visiting medics nor the staff in the home ever suspected that they would be the carriers of Covid. Mount Joseph had been very diligent in their efforts to keep the virus out of the home, restricting visits to family only, ensuring that all who entered had themselves been vaccinated, and that they all wore masks. They prided themselves in telling families of their continued success. Many other such retirement homes had had to close because of the virus. Residents had to be moved to other facilities. There had been a horrific degree of fatalities amongst the aged in retirement homes. A scandal that was all over the press. But Mount Joseph looked upon the medics as being above suspicion, experienced in their diligence, their procedures, and restrictions had been relaxed for them.

Just after dinner, and before she began to feel unwell, Tom, her neighbour in Ballyboe, had come to visit her, but, although his face was familiar, she didn't know who he was. He had to sit outside her window and talk to her via a telephone. Nurse Radley had helped translate and tell her about Tom and what he was saying to her. Radley had told her that, because he was not immediate family he was not allowed to come in. Tom had tried to be cheerful and make small talk, but all she could think of was about when he would leave so she could go to bed and sleep.

He seemed a nice man. Very old, though. He's the sort you'd expect to be living is this place, not coming to visit. He talked a lot about Ballyboe. Now, I know that place, I know the name, very well, but I just can't picture in my head where on earth it is. He had brought a dog with him. Stella, wasn't that what he said was the name of the dog. We used to have a dog just like that. Now….what was the dog's name? Can't remember. I'd loved to have had the dog in the room, petting and rubbing it, but that bitch of a nurse said no.

I haven't seen Jim for some time now. He must be busy. I asked that fellow, that old fellow, if he had seen Jim in his travels. He smiled and said he hadn't.

Helina

Helina holds tightly onto Tenen's hand as they make their way through the busy streets. You must hold my hand all the time, she has said to him. Hashim is leading the way, the elder boy, Omer, refusing to take anybody's hand. Even though she is already eighteen years old she has never been to Addis Ababa before. In fact, she has rarely been away from Lalibela. The furthest she has ever travelled is to Gondar. She went there once with her mother. From what she has seen so far of her capital city, she doesn't like it. Too many people. A maize of narrow streets. But Hashim has said that the safest way for them to move in the city is through the busy streets, mingling with the crowds. Out in the open, or in a taxi, they are more likely to be stopped. There are soldiers everywhere. Hashim has told us all that if we are stopped the boys must not speak. Soldiers will take them away if they know they are foreigners.

Her gabi is soiled from all the travelling. She has not had any time to wash clothes. The boys' clothes too are ragged. Hashim got them from friends. They all look like paupers. But Hashim says that is best. If they are clean and well-dressed they will stand out. Helina has noticed many shops in Addis with colourful habesha kemis. She would love to have one of them for the meeting with the boys' uncle. She wants to make an impression on him. She wants him to recognise that she is good to the boys, that the boys need her.

Ireland – she only has a vague impression of where it is and how far away it is. Mary, the boys' mother, told her it was further west than England, but she doesn't even know where that is. Two years ago her mother got a job in the bakery in Lalibela. The man who owns it was called Dezy, but his full name was Desalgn Gebire Giorgis. He told the people that the oven for the bakery was funded by a kind Christian man from Ireland. Before that nobody had ever even heard about Ireland. But then the war started and the soldiers from Tigray came. The electricity was cut off, so the bakery had to close. They had sourced and were buying a generator, also funded by the kind man from Ireland, when Lalibela was bombed and the bakery building was demolished.

As she negotiates her way through the streets, trying not to lose sight of Hashim, dodging the incessant motor bicycles that plough through the pedestrians, Helina touches her midriff to check that the linen waist band she has around her is still there. She has been warned that Addis is a place where thieves could steal even your underwear without you being aware of it. The waist band has the boys' passports in it, as well as her own Keble card. She had examined them in the toilet this morning. Her Keble card is an Ethiopian identity card, with her photograph on it. It shows that Helina Belay Berham was born on the third day of January 2004. Only her name is written in English; all of the other insertions are in Amharic. The Keble card cost me two hundred birr. That was, for me, the wages of one week. I couldn't afford a passport. That cost many times what a Keble card cost.

Inati, that's what I call my mother, told me before I left, not to tell anyone, especially Habtamu, and not even Hashim, about the boys' passports. They are most valuable, and if anyone finds out about them money will have to be paid to get them back. Omer knows that I have the passports, but he has promised me that he won't tell anyone, even Tenen.

Amare was the first one of our family to leave Ethiopia. Inati says he had to, because he wanted to give up his religion. Everyone in Ethiopia goes to church and prays. Inati didn't know where Amare got his ideas from. She said he was just confused, and that he would be back. We all prayed for him to come back to Lalibela and go to church again. But Amare said he couldn't. I don't know why he went to Ireland. Why so far away? He was gone for ten years. Then he did came back. With his Irish wife and two children. I think it was Mary really who wanted to come and live in Lalibela. I think she wanted to do what she called charity work here.

We loved to sit and listen to Amare tell us about Ireland. He said it was a windy green island where it rains a lot. They have never had a drought in Ireland. Can you imagine? A country that has never had a drought. So, it is my dream to go there. Maybe I will live there. And get married. Maybe I will marry the boys' uncle. Wouldn't that be great. I'm sure the boys would like that.

I loved Mary. She was so kind. Even though she didn't believe in God. I had never met anyone before that didn't believe in God. Except, of course, Amare. How can you not believe in God? But I don't believe what our priest said, that what happened to Amare and her was a punishment from God. I don't believe that for a minute. She was just an angel. She taught me English, and she showed me how to cook Irish food. Now I can make shepherd's pie, and I can cook an Irish stew.

Inati told me not to tell the boys that their mother is dead. That is a matter for the boys' family, and not you, she said. They will tell the boys when they feel that the time is right. Perhaps they won't be told until they are safely back in Ireland. Those poor little lads have been through such trauma, so much hardship, first losing their father, and then seeing soldiers dragging their mother away. Nobody knows what effect it would have on them to tell them that their mother is dead, never coming back.

All of us in Lalibela know that Mary suffered a cruel time in prison before the Tigrayans killed her. I heard the details. Horrible. But Inati told me not to talk to the boys' family about it. She says it would look too badly on Ethiopia for the details to get out. We are not animals in Ethiopia, we are good people. But the Tigrayans, they are animals.

Habtamu, but his friends call him Tamu. I'm not a friend, so I don't, he is a Tigrayan. But he has lived in

Lalibela nearly all his life. One day we will drive the Tigrayans out of Lalibela, and we will drive Habtamu with them. He is such a bad man. He took the boys away in his big truck. He said he was going to protect them. I wanted to go with them, but he said no. It was only when I told him that he wouldn't be able to talk to them, that they only spoke English, that he agreed to take me as well. He took us into the hills to his farm. Everywhere around his farm there are gum trees. Habtamu grows them, then cuts them down to make long poles which he sells. Trucks are coming to his farm to buy these long poles. I had to help with them. They are very heavy and difficult to get into the trucks.

One evening Habtamu took me into the forest of his gum trees. He said he wanted to show me something, but I was really afraid of him, and I didn't want to go. He said if I didn't go with him then I could leave and go home. So, I went with him. But I only followed him and stayed a safe distance behind. I knew what he wanted, so I was ready. When he stopped in the middle of the forest and turned towards me, I knew what was going to happen. As he reached for me, I turned and ran away. He ran after me, telling me to stop. But I didn't. When we got back to his yard I thought he was going to tell me to go home, so, I hid from him. But, next morning he said nothing. Thanks God he has not tried anything again.

Habtamu was really mad when the Ethiopian soldiers came and took his two sons away. That was last year, when the war was getting started. His sons were made to join into the army. They didn't want to fight against other Tigrayans. I heard that they left and ran away from the army and went north into the heart of Tigray. Maybe they even joined the Tigray soldiers. If Lalibela ever is free again those two boys better not come back. I didn't like them anyway.

Poor Amare. He didn't want to have anything to do with the war. He had packed up all the family's stuff, and they were about to leave to go back to Ireland, but the elders in the town said he should stay and fight. They wouldn't allow him to leave. So he agreed to help, but only working as a clerk, not fighting. But when the Tigrayans entered the town they took him like all the rest, and he was shot.

Habtamu now has his money and he is gone, thanks God. He wanted a million birr for each of the boys, but Hashim told him that he would only get a million for them both. Habtamu said that he had to pay the army general in Lalibela a big amount to give him the paper for us to get to Addis. I heard him talking, and I told Hashim that the amount he needed to pay for the paper was one hundred thousand. So, Habtamu is now a rich man. He wouldn't give Hashim the paper. Whatever was on it Habtamu was able to show it at every army checkpoint, and we were all allowed safely through. I don't know why he didn't then give Hashim the paper. Maybe he needs it to get back to Lalibela.

Leaving Lalibela, and maybe leaving Ethiopia, will be the biggest change to my life. But it is something I have been dreaming about ever since I was a child. My twin brother, Anwar, and I talked about it a lot. Before we left Inati kissed me goodbye and said I should be happy to go to Ireland. There is no life for me, she said, either in Lalibela or anywhere else in Ethiopia. She said I could send her money when I am working in Ireland. I pray to God that this happens.

Anwar wants me to try and get him also to Ireland. But I'm not sure about that. I will tell you, Anwar is very different from me. He is always trying to make money. And he doesn't care how he makes it. He buys things and then wants to sell them at a higher price. He has a mobile phone that he is always looking at. And he has an Email address. Anwar comes up to tourists on the street and tells them he would like to write to them. It is supposed to be to improve his English. Often the tourist agree. Anwar now has ten, or maybe more, people who he writes to. But he is not trying to improve his English. This is Anwar's trick. When he has written to them a few times he starts telling them lies, in order to get money out of them. He says he wants to go to college. Or he makes up a sad story about the family. If Inati knew about this she would punish him. That is why I would be scared to have Anwar with me in Ireland. He might ruin everything for me.

Peter

The Passenger Control Hall at Addis Ababa airport was simply a comical, chaotic melee. Analogous to a rugby maul, where every member of the teams was involved. Peter could see three queues, the first a rather short one, the others much longer. People were pressing forward, holding papers above their heads, shouting, many of them ignoring the queue, with loud arguments raging. Naturally, Peter chose the shortest queue. Wrong decision. When he reached the end of it he realised that it was for people to hand in their payment receipt and get their visas stamped onto the passport. There were no directional signs, no officials or airport staff to ask questions of. Frustrated, Peter looked for someone, anyone, who could speak English. The trouble was that the majority of the those in the hall were dressed in Arabic or African dress. He tried a large man in white robes. No English. A woman in what looked to him like Nigerian costume was also of no help.

Finally, he spotted a grey suit, obviously a man from the civilised west. The gentleman was small and bespectacled, and he appeared to be scared of coming into contact with anyone. When Peter approached him he instinctively backed away, lifting his hand to ensure that his mask was tight to the bridge of his nose.

"I wonder if you can help me?" Peter began. But a set of scared eyes just peered back at him. "I don't know which queue to go to. I want to get my visa."

"Ah, Engleesh," the little, well-dressed, man suddenly came alive. "Vot can I do for you?"

Sounds like a German....or possibly an Austrian.

"You have to go to zhat counter over zhere and fill in the wisa application," the German advised. "Zen you join zis queue. Zhey will examine your documents and stamp ze form, zen you go to zhat queue. Zhat queue is for paying. After you have paid you come to zis, the final queue."

"Very confusing."

"Ya, sure. The Ethiopian way of getting money from ze tourists. Zhey don't trust those in the first office to handle ze money. Only those in the second, where, you will see, zere is a man with a gun." Peter looked at the man, dressed in army uniform, holding a sub-machine gun.

Of course, he should have known. After all, he was a professional travel writer. And, after all, he had been to this airport before, albeit more than ten years ago. He should have applied for his visa on-line before he left Ireland. Stupid. But he had been too busy. Busy fending off the press – now the national newspapers were chasing the story of the ransom – busy getting ready, busy buying all of the things Denise said he would need.

What a wonderfully organised woman Denise is. It would never have crossed my mind that i should buy clothes for the boys, shoes of the correct sizes (how would i know the size of the boys' feet?), that they would need books and little games to amuse them on the flight home, snacks – children have to be fed every two hours max, she had said – a soft toy for them to cuddle.

Denise has been, I dunno, different, in the last few days. Talking a lot, being, what should I say, very chatty, asking endless questions. Then she was really insistent on meeting Tom Draper. As it happens, I need Tom's help when the boys come. So, we had him to dinner in my house. They got along really well together. And Tom was only too happy to protect us from the paparazzi. He will guard the gate, tell callers lies, if he has to, mind and walk Stella. The three of us concocted a plan of campaign: I will not fly back to Dublin with the boys; rather I will fly in to Cork, via Paris; Tom is going to pick us up in Cork; I will tell Paul that I will be coming in to Dublin airport on Friday afternoon; Denise will tell the same to her neighbour, May; and Tom will tell anyone he meets, especially those massing at the gate, the same arrangement; however, by Thursday evening the boys and I will be safely in the house in Ballyboe, with the gate locked.

But, then Denise wanted to talk about Tchaikovsky. Not Mozart or Beethoven or Shostakovich, just Tchaikovsky. She seemed to know a lot about him. Well, I have the biography of the Russian on my shelf, a biography I found fascinating. Of course, he would be one of my favourites. Tom's too. As soon as we exhausted Tchaikovsky, she quickly moved the conversation from there to literature, specifically to Colm Tobin. It was like she was a compere interviewing us about aspects of art. I didn't know she was a fan and had read so many of his books. The two I liked best were *The Blackwater Lightship* and *Brooklyn.* I found his life-story of Thomas Mann in *The Magician* boring and repetitive. Tom's not a reader, well, not a reader of fiction, so he was a bit lost in this phase of the conversation. I could see he was tiring, so we called it a night.

After I had seen Tom out to the gate and discussed how we might make it more private I checked and double-checked my suitcase and travel documents before retiring. I thought Denise would by then be fast asleep, but, no, I found her sitting up in the bed reading. Stark naked. She wanted to talk. Well, talk first, I deduced.

"Tom is a nice man," she said.

"Ah, he's the salt of the earth. He's been a great friend and neighbour since my father and mother moved us to Ballyboe. You know he's taking me to the airport? He always does when I go on a trip."

"I didn't realise that he was that old."

"Yeah, he's pushing eighty."

"And he never married?"

I didn't answer that. I assume most people know that Tom is gay. I could have told her about his partner, Kevin, but I just wanted to go asleep.

I was gone for a while, brushing my teeth and putting on my pyjamas, but when I came back to the bed she was still awake. When she reached to open my pyjama top her need to have intercourse was crystal clear. Well, I was tired after a long day, and a bit intoxicated, but I felt I had to make the effort. It's all very well for women in these situations. They are not burdened with any essential requirement for intercourse, if you know what I mean. But we men are. Maybe I should investigate erectile medication. Wonder if it works? The session wasn't entirely fulfilling. Awkward and clumsy. But I believe that at least I satisfied her, even if I never myself reached a climax.

Just as I was nodding off to sleep Denise muses, "Peter, what's going to happen to the boys when they arrive? I mean, they no longer have a mother or a father. Presumably they will live here with you? You will become their new father. And mother?"

Well, Denise and I have been over this before. And here we go again. It seems that she asks me a question; if she doesn't get the answer she wants, she lets the matter lie. Then, a week or so later she drums up the same question. What does she want me to say? All I was concerned with was rescuing them, bringing them back to Ireland. I never thought much about what happens after that. Boarding school was my first thought. I mean, I have to get back to work. They're now orphans. Nothing anyone can do about it. I never had that innate compulsion to be a father. Yeah, I'll be their guardian, but fatherhood would be a big step for me. And, no doubt, for them.

"Yeah, I suppose they will have to stay here in Ballyboe for some time until we sort things out."

"And then?"

"Don't know."

He closed his eyes and pretended to be falling asleep, but he knew that the boys' future was something he would have to come back to, to resolve, sooner or later. For the moment he would focus on Ethiopia and the venture ahead.

After Peter had checked in to his hotel and arranged his room he went out into the forecourt for some fresh air. There he found the little German sitting outside on an armchair reading a newspaper.

"Ah, ze Engleesh got his wisa."

"Actually, Irish, not English."

"Same thing."

"Same as Germans and Austrians?"

"No, no, we Germans are much different from the Austrians."

"And we Irish are poles apart from the English. The only thing we have in common, just as you and the Austrians, is language."

"Okay, okay. I zee."

Peter didn't really want to chat, but the little German was eager. As he opened up to the Irishman Peter couldn't help noticing a long hair protruding from the German's left earlobe. It was all of two centimetres long. He would have liked to reach out and pluck it. Now, you might do that to a close friend, or a brother, but you certainly wouldn't do it to a stranger, and definitely not a German. The little man had changed from the grey suit to bright coloured casuals, from black, polished shoes to brown sandals with light brown socks. Now that he was unmasked Peter could put his age in the early sixties. So, sixty-year old German, unmarried (a wife would surely have plucked the earlobe hair), here in Addis working (no tourists during the pandemic, not to mention the war). Peter was congratulation himself of his fine detective work, when the German confirmed that he was a diplomat, out in Ethiopia to monitor how the EC aid was being spent. So, correct on the first count.

"My wife said there was no way she was coming. Too dangerous because of the war and the pandemic." Well, wrong on the second count.

"And what ez the Engleesh, ……. sorry, Ireesh, doing in Addis Ababa? Surely not on holiday?" With the question the little man proffered one of his cards. Jurgen Paul Schneider was a counsellor with the EC.

Peter decided that there was nothing to be lost from confiding in his new friend. So, he told all. It had crossed his mind that, if he got into trouble with immigration, having a diplomat as a friend might be helpful, especially one who was monitoring aid to the country.

"Might I suggest," the German advised, "that, if the boys have the same family name as you, that you tell everyone here in Ethiopia that they are your sons."

"That's a great idea."

Why didn't I think of that? Brilliant. It cuts out awkward questions, not just in Ethiopia, but on entry to Ireland too.

"If you are not otherwise engaged, perhaps we might have dinner together?" Peter suggested.

"Delighted," the Counsellor replied.

They ate a Western-style meal in the hotel restaurant, accompanied by an Ethiopian wine.

"I didn't know that Ethiopia produced vines," Jurgen said, approvingly sipping from his glass.

"Viniculture in Ethiopia dates back two thousand years," Peter began his little speech, "although it became moribund with the advance of religion. It was only as late as the nineteen-fifties that serious production returned. In the Rift Valley, where this particular bottle comes from, they have ideal conditions – climate and soil. Indeed, the climate allows them to make two harvests every year."

"Wery interesting," the German said, but Peter could see that his companion was not really a wine person.

Immediately after dinner Peter had to lie down. He was feeling particularly jaded after the journey and the arrival in Addis. He had a tickly cough and a headache. Could be the African dust. Must get some medicine for this cough, but where would I get it in Addis Ababa? He had no problem falling into a deep sleep.

Peter was shaving, making himself ready for the day ahead, when the hotel phone rang.

"Mister Sheridan?"

"Yes."

"There is a man on the telephone for you. His name is Hashim."

Hashim's voice was excited, to the point of being frantic. "Mister Peter, we are here in Addis. Me, the boys and Helina. We are in my cousin's house not too far from your hotel…."

"Okay, okay, bring them to the hotel."

"No, no, Mister Peter. There are soldiers outside your hotel. I went there and saw them. They will stop us. If they discover that the boys are not Ethiopian they will surely take them."

"Wait, wait, let me think……..by the way, who is Helina?"

"Helina is my cousin. She has been with the boys all the time."

"Okay, okay, I will come to you. I will bring the boys clothes. Then the boys and I will come to the hotel, and the boys will act as my children. Give me your address and I will come."

Peter was about to leave the hotel when a second telephone call came. This time it was from Ireland. The tragic news was that Covid had somehow infiltrated the nursing home that his mother was in. Nurse Radley told him that Anne was one of several who had contracted the virus and that she was quite sick. Peter immediately rang Paul.

"Hello!"

"Have you been up to the nursing home today?"

"Yeah, I was there this morning. Everything is fine."

"Oh, yeah? You little bastard. You dirty liar. Mam has Covid. She's very sick. You get your sorry ass up there and look in on her. And text me back about it."

Omer

Tenen is fast asleep. He has been asleep now for over an hour, falling quickly into oblivion soon after the take-off from Addis Ababa. His deep slumber reflects the harrowing time he has had over the past few weeks. In his window seat he slumps, mouth wide open, his hands clutching the cuddly lamb that Peter had brought for him. Omer, by contrast is wide awake, reading one of the new books. He hasn't once closed his eyes. Even when Peter dozed Omer continued to be active.

This is a great book. The letters are big, so I can see them easily, and there are no long words. But the book would be no good for Tenen, 'cause there are not many pictures, and Tenen can't read. It was Mama who taught me to read. But I haven't read, or even seen, a book for a long time. This book is called *My First Book of Bedtime Stories.* There are six parts to the book, and each part has ten stories. So that's ......sixty stories. You see, I am good with numbers as well. There are two hundred and five pages in the book. I have already read thirty-one pages. This story is about a family of goats who live in the forest. The mama goat has to go to the shop, so she tells the children – there are seven young goats – not to open the door or the wolf will get in. But the wolf tricks them and gets in, and he swallows them all except one. Then the mama goat comes home and she butts the wolf so hard that he has to cough up the children.

Uncle Peter came to the house in Addis to collect us. The house was a grotty place, with chickens coming into it. There was chicken shit all over the floor. Outside in the yard there were hundreds of empty plastic bottles.

It was wonderful to see Uncle Peter, and I gave him a big cuddle. Tenen didn't give him any cuddle. But he never met Helina before, and he didn't know who she was. Uncle Peter just wanted to take us back to the hotel, and he didn't want to take Helina, but I said that Helina should come. She had helped us through the long journey through Ethiopia. And she wants to come to Ireland. She would like to live with us. I think that would be great. Mama would be pleased if Helina was with us. I think Uncle Peter changed his mind, first of all when Tenen went over and took Helina's hand, but then Helina lifted her dress and took out the passports from the pooch she had strapped around her belly. Uncle Peter was very pleased with the passports.

Uncle Peter gave us new clothes that he had brought from Ireland. I was glad to get the Ethiopian clothes off. They were dirty and smelly. But the trousers he bought for me are a bit short. He said that I had grown very tall.

Then Uncle Peter told me and Tenen that we should call him Papa. He said that the soldiers might take us away from him if they thought we weren't his children. It was funny. Uncle Peter tells us to call him Papa, then he asks

Tenen who he is and Tenen says Uncle Peter. No, says Uncle Peter, you have to say, if anybody asks, that I'm your father. So, a second time he asks Tenen who he is and Tenen looks at me. He didn't know what to do. So, I whispered to Tenen, *"we don't have a father, but we do have Uncle Peter. So, why don't we call Uncle Peter Papa."* And then, d'you know what happened? Tenen says to Uncle Peter "do you want to be our new Papa?" Well, Uncle Peter was very surprised, but he said, "okay, I'm gonna be your Papa." So, he says to Tenen, "who am I?" and Tenen says, "you're our new Papa." We all laughed. Even Tenen laughed, but I don't think he knew why we were laughing. "No," says Uncle Peter, "not your new Papa, just your Papa." I think Tenen got it, 'cause now he only calls him Papa.

Uncle Peter also told us what to do if anyone starts asking questions. He said we should start to whinge and come over and hold his leg, crying "Papa, Papa." We thought that was ever so funny, but we didn't have to do it. The soldiers outside the hotel just looked at our passports and let us go. Then, at the airport, when people looked at our passports they didn't ask any questions. Tenen had been practicing whinging, just in case. He's funny when he pretends to cry, 'cause he always has a smile on his face.

We all thought that Hashim was great. He knows the big city of Addis Ababa very well. We would be going along one street and Hashim would stop. "Wait," he would say, "soldiers." Then he would take us through shops and narrow lanes out to the next street. I was afraid. We were all afraid. But it was exciting too. Once we were in a street and two soldiers came along. Hashim told us to look at the things they were selling in the shop. And the soldiers passed us by without seeing us.

We are very sad that Helina couldn't come. She has no passport. Uncle Peter wanted to bring her. But his friend at the hotel told him that he wouldn't be allowed. Uncle Peter wanted her to come to Ireland as a refugee. I don't know what a refugee is. The friend in the hotel promised that he would get Helina a passport and that he would make sure that she was able to come to Ireland. I think Mama is coming in a few days to Addis – that's what Helina said – and Helina said that she would come to Ireland with Mama.

We are flying over Africa. And then we will fly to Paris. That's in France. It's not fair that Tenen got the seat at the window. He's just lying there fast asleep. I wanted the window seat. Then I could look out at all the lights in the cities down under us. Uncle Peter says that we are to share the window seat, but Tenen has been in it for a long time now, and he's just sleeping. I wanted to move him, but Uncle Peter said no, that we mustn't wake him. I gave his leg a good kick to try and wake him, but it didn't. It's just not fair.

We just had time to eat dinner before the taxi came to take us to the airport. Uncle Peter asked us were we hungry, and I said that we were starving. "Starving," he said. Then he asked us what did we want to eat. We both said the same word together. Chips. So we got burgers and chips, with tomato ketchup. And we each got a big glass of Coca Cola. And then we had ice cream. It was wonderful. And Uncle Peter said that, when we get to his house, he will fry us sausages. No more yukky Ethiopian food.

When we get to Uncle Peter's house the first thing I'm going to do is to go outside and kick football. I hope Uncle Peter has a football. But, if he hasn't, I'm sure he will buy me one. Maybe my friend, Tony, will be around to play. And we can play with Stella too.

Tom

Tom's favourite cigarette is with a cup of tea after breakfast. This morning he is trying to manage the cup in one hand, an umbrella in the other and switching the cigarette and cup between the two. He is on gate duty. Manning the locked gate to Ballyboe House to keep unwanted intruders out. He is admiring his handiwork. Whilst Peter was in Ethiopia Tom has fixed vertical timbers to both sides of the gate to afford privacy to the garden. Now the paparazzi can't even see into the property.

It was feckin mayhem here for nearly a week. Me working on them slats for the gate, a hape of them annoying me with endless questions. When are the boys coming home? Has the ransom been paid? Can you give us some background on the case? No, I feckin can't. Now bugger off and let me get on with me work. I was even offered a cash reward by one enterprising fella for information.

After a week of dry, settled weather the rain has returned, sheets of it being driven almost horizontally by strong winds. But Tom welcomes the rain. This time. The plants need it. They have been starved of water for weeks. He wanders around examining shrubs and flowers, and is pleased to see that the clearest evidence of late spring is upon us, buds opening, the daffodils in full bloom, the bluebells and garlic dancing in the wind. Tom has been a gardener all his long life. Many of the plants here in Ballyboe date back to when he and his father planted them, all of fifty years ago. He looks at the Norway maple and marvels at its fine structure and big leaves. The yew tree on the side of the drive he planted with his own hands, having transplanted it as a sapling taken from the yew forest in Killarney.

It was a sad day when he had to sell Ballyboe, to leave this garden and move to the farm cottage down the lane. Ballyboe had been his home. His home until he was in his thirties. The home of the Drapers for countless years. *Baile an Bhó*, the home of the cow, or maybe it's *Baile na mBó*, the home of the cows? I've lost much of the Irish I learned. Anyway, this lane was once an artery to the west, one of the roads to Galway. But the end had to come. When his mother passed away his siblings, Michael, Paddy and Josie, wanted their share. They're all dead now. I'm the last of the Drapers of Ballyboe. If only my father had had the same foresight as Jim Sheridan, setting out in his will that the house should always remain in the Draper family. That would mean that one of Josie's children would have to come home and live in it.

But, I'm content with my little cottage. Sure, what more would a single man want? But, it is looking like there might have to be two of us sharing the house soon. Kevin is becoming more and more shuck, unable to look after himself. We have talked about him moving in with me. He was reluctant at first, but he's gradually coming 'round to it. Now that I'm over the Covid, if indeed I ever had it (you can't surely trust them feckin test things), I'll push him to move.

I have the big field next to me. We always knew it as the fuchsia field, because it is surrounded by bushes of fuchsia. It's nearly two acres of flat ground. You wouldn't believe how many people have come and asked to buy that field. Sure, I'd have no use for the money. And Johnny Mac from up the road is always asking if I'd set the field, let him graze his horse in there. No, feck it, I'd rather let the field for the wildlife. I can stroll in there of a morning and marvel at the bees humming, maybe the odd fox hiding in the long grass. When I was a child there used to be corncrakes in that field. Sadly the corncrakes are long gone. Cutting the grass is what caused their departure. But, maybe, just maybe, one day they will return. That's why I don't cut the grass. Haven't cut it for years now.

And, well, we couldn't have picked a better family to mind the place. Jim Sheridan, and now Peter, have kept and enhanced the garden. The gravel drive hasn't a weed in it; perimeter hedges are regularly trimmed; bark mulch is spread between the shrubs every spring; plants are methodically thinned out, and the box garden is as good today as it was when his father laid it out. Peter and he often walk the property, discussing what needs to be done. He worked with Peter when it was decided to turn the briar-covered patch in the lower area into an orchard. Now the patch boasts ten fruit trees, bushes of blackcurrants, rhubarb, raspberries, gooseberries and blueberries. None of the fruit is harvested. It is all for the birds. In the autumn the blackbirds will gorge themselves on the blackcurrants and wipe them out in a morning. Sure, I might not have kept the place any better than the Sheridans have done.

That's a nice little car Peter has. Electric. I was seriously thinking of getting an electric car. That's if I could afford it, which is rather unlikely. But, then, coming back from Cork with Peter and the boys, didn't he say that his electric one would have had to be charged at least once en route. Half an hour hanging about waiting for the thing to boot up. Feck that!

Tom's musings are interrupted by noises from outside the gate. Peering through the new slats he sees the big Volvo arriving. He knows that Paul is here.

"What the fuck!" he hears Paul exclaim. Tom smiles to himself. That bastard has been a pain in my arse ever since he came to Ballyboe. How can two brothers be so different? Peter, a kind and gentle man, and his brother a conniving blackguard. When the lad was only a gosson Tom couldn't pass along the lane without Paul and his friends mocking. A hape of them would be up on the ditch shouting disgusting things at me. *Go on ya dirty queer! D'ya want ta suck me cock?* Well, I won't stand for any nonsense from him now.

Paul begins to rattle the gate, muttering profanities as his does so. I'd better stop him.

"Sorry, nobody is allowed in."

There is a pause, and then Paul shouts, "is that you Tom?" Oh, so it's Tom now, not the dirty queer.

"Yes, Paul, Peter gave me instructions that nobody was to come in."

"Lookit, this house is as much mine as it is Peter's. I need to talk to my brother about our mother. Open the fuckin gate."

"Everyone in the house is asleep. And, anyway, the house is full of Covid. I think they all have it. If you want to give me a message for Peter I'll see he gets it. Otherwise I suggest you ring Peter later in the morning and talk to him."

Paul issues a distinctive "fuck" before he retreats from the rain and starts up his car.

As Tom listens to the engine puttering back up the lane he hears the door of the house open. Stella comes tearing out, barking excitedly. The dog comes to Tom, wagging her tail and wanting to be rubbed. Denise appears in her nightgown.

"Who was that, Tom?"

"It was Peter's brother, Paul. A bit annoyed that I wouldn't let him in."

"Well done, Tom. D'you want to come in for a bit of breakfast?"

I'm a bit wary of this Englishwoman. She's pleasant, but nobody is going to walk over her. She's her own woman, if you know what I mean. I wouldn't say bossy, but definitely no pushover. Somehow, I can't see Peter putting up with her, that's on a long term basis. Peter likes his own ways. He's not a social animal. Quiet and happy with his own company. You know the type. But this Englishwoman is a little in-your-face. Still, Peter is going to need a lot of help now with them two gossons. She has a little girl. Maybe she's good with children. And her little girl might be a nice child for the gossons to play with. I'd say that Peter will be lost otherwise. That dinner we had before Peter went off, well, I knew she was fishing, asking endless questions. She knew damn well that Tchaikovsky was gay, then she goes on to Colm Tobin. I could see that Peter didn't twig. But I did. I knew what she was up to. She has to know that I am gay. I was tempted to say "why don't you come out with it. Just ask us what our attitude is to homosexuality?" Ah, mebbe I'm being harsh on her. Mebbe she's alright. We'll see.

"I won't come in, ma'am, I'm too wet." I'd rather stay out here on guard.

"Ah, don't be silly. Take those wet clothes off and come on in."

I'll just go in and have a cup of tae. What about the Covid? Peter thinks he has it. Jaysus, maybe I gave it to him on the trip to Dublin. Even though he can't give it back to me, I don't want to be a carrier. I have to think of Kevin. Ah, feck it, what's the harm.

The house was bustling. Children seemed to be running everywhere. The dog, with its wet paws, was barking with excitement, scampering from one to the other. Peter, with a mask on, was busy over a frying pan in the kitchen. The noise subsided somewhat when Tom appeared.

"Morning, Tom," Peter called.

"Still wearing the mask, I see," Tom replied.

"Yeah, can't take it off until the boss says so." He looked over at Denise.

"We are all doing antigen tests later this morning. We'll get you a tester as well."

That'll be interesting. To see if the second test confirms I am well over it.

"How is your mother?"

"She's very poorly, Tom. They can't be confident that she'll pull out of this damn virus. I was up there this morning. Doesn't look good."

"Oh, I'm sorry about that."

The smallest boy, what was his name, Tenden, or something, was sucking the two middle fingers on his right hand. He was tightly holding a woolly lamb under his arm. He looked at Tom, remembering that it was he who drove them the long journey from Cork, and ventured a reticent smile. The bigger boy, Omer, was on the floor in the living room, with a card game laid out before him. But he wasn't concentrating on it; he was jumping and running around. Denise's little girl was skipping about humming to herself, Stella hopping in unison. A once quiet house, where you could sit and chat quietly, was transformed into a hub of commotion.

Isn't it great to hear the squeals of little children.

Can you imagine them two gossons going to school here in Mullingar. What's your name? Tenden. What? Tenden. What kind of a name is that? And Omer, well, what will the other children make of those quare names? Maybe they should just change them to Ted and Ollie.

"I won't stop," Tom protested, "I'd better get back to the gate."

"Sit down and have a cup of tea and a sausage," said Peter, "the gate can wait. Anyway, there won't be anyone out there in the rain."

"Well, your brother was there a minute ago. He was very put out that I wouldn't open the gate for him. Said he wanted to talk to you about Anne."

"Now, Tom," Peter stopped turning sausages and came over, "of all the people to keep out, Paul is the most important. I don't want that fellow in here on any account. I'll tell you why later."

You don't have to tell me. The world can't have any interface with the boys until they have been told, and have gotten over, the fact that their mother is dead. Poor craters.

As Tom drank his tea he noticed that the little boy was continually watching him. He would just sit there staring, or move around the table, but, all the time, the two little eyes peered out from behind the woolly lamb, focused on Tom. Tom had a few tricks he could perform with his hands; losing his left thumb, then his right; drumming his fingers so that his nails made a repetitive drumroll; making a coin in his hand suddenly disappear. He carried these out silently, with only the boy watching. Everyone else in the house was preoccupied. The boy began to take an interest. He seemed to be particularly intrigued by the disappearing coin. Tom proffered the coin, but the boy wouldn't take it. So, Tom performed the trick again. This time the boy came closer and reached to open Tom's hand, expecting to find the coin concealed there. When Tom showed him the coin, now in the other hand, the boy smiled.

"D'you want me to show you how it's done?"

The boy nodded.

"You'll have to promise never to tell anybody."

The boy nodded again, this time with a wide smile. Tom had established a connection with him. Exactly the same way, many years ago, when he established a connection with Peter. I seem to have a way with little boys.

Denise

Denise has had to call time on her job in the Wine emporium. Her life had steadily taken on a new momentum. Peter's nephews would require her full-time attention for the foreseeable future. Jerome had been very understanding. Of course, she couldn't spell out the details for him, just to say that she was badly needed in Ballyboe with the return of the two boys.

"Yes, yes, of course, I completely understand," he had said, "just let me know if there is anything I can do to help. And your job will be here whenever you're available again. And give Peter my best regards."

She had settled the children so that she could retreat with her tablet and mobile to the bedroom. Television. Children will always look at it. Not good for them, of course, but, under the circumstances, it was the only way to bring a period of calm into the house. A calm so that she could retreat to the bedroom. The boys had not seen a television for a long time, let alone watched it. And Audrey, well, the girl would happily watch anything on the telly. She was keenly aware that she would have to get back to them as quickly as possible. And there was another task for the day: Nan's birthday was coming up, and she would have to get Audrey to make a card for it. Must continue to cultivate the relationship between Audrey and her grandmother.

I'm sure Peter has the Covid. He doesn't know where and when he picked it up, if he indeed did pick it up. He thought he was a bit chesty when he landed in Addis Ababa, but the symptoms weren't really that bad. He has been wearing that bloody mask since he landed in Ireland. Sex, of course, was out of the question. At least until he knows whether he has the virus or not. I suppose it's the sensible thing to do. But it's very difficult to hold back and keep your distance from someone whom you haven't seen for nearly a week, someone who is part of your life, who you want to touch, to cuddle, to kiss.

Poor little Tenen. The child was obviously in a state of trauma. He was listless, not interested in what the other two were up to, clinging to that precious little woollen lamb, continually sucking his fingers. She had tried various distractions – read a story, make something with the Lego, line up the dolls and teddies and fantasise with them. All to no avail; nothing worked. She wanted to cuddle him, but he withdrew. "I want my mama," he painfully whispered. But, did you see that Tom fellow? How he has struck up a rapport with the boy. He's a really nice man, that Tom. There he was doing tricks with Tenen, and the next time I looked he had the boy up on his knee, drumming his fingers on the table. Now, others (I'm thinking of May) would be scared to see a little boy on the knee of a homosexual, but I'm not in the least.

I see very clearly now Peter's limitations; he is useless when it comes to children; in a crisis he panics, unable to think straight. There he is downstairs more concerned with keeping the place tidy than in concentrating on what is important. Why can't he see that the children's mental peace is paramount. I will simply have to adopt the role of leader. But, I will have to do it subtlety, with tact. Make out that he is actually making the key decisions. Let him off tidying and cleaning, so long as he doesn't start imposing restrictions. He told me that Tenen is calling him Papa, but I have yet to witness that. Well, at least he had the foresight not to tell the boys that their mother was dead. Not yet. The way has to be paved out first. At least he had the common sense to see that.

But his attitude to this girl, Helina, was just appalling. To him she was a distraction, a nuisance. We have enough on our plates than to be bringing an Ethiopian young adolescent into the house as well, he said. He couldn't see any benefit in bringing her to Ballyboe. Imagine! It took me a while to show him that Helina would be, as the Irish say, a godsend. She would be a vital link between the boys and their parents; they had lived with her for some years now; they were used to her; she could also be a great help in the house when he and I would have to go to work.

I'd be reasonably confident that Peter is heterosexual. Reasonably, not fully. But, does it really matter? It seems to me that he and Tom are just great friends, nothing more. But, then, I couldn't be totally sure.

They had sat up late into the night talking. The boys had to be told, sooner or later, that their mother was dead, that she wasn't ever coming back. But when, and how to tell them? Should they seek professional help? Or just face up to it and tell them straight? Well, that was Peter's proposal. The worry of it kept her from sleeping, and occupied her head from the moment she awoke.

She was Googling *Child Psychologists Ireland.* If she was going to find one it had to be today. There would be little hope tomorrow, Saturday, and no hope at all on Sunday. How do you engage someone without first knowing that they are trustworthy, that they won't spill the news to someone else? Can you imagine the headlines *Returned Children Not Aware Their Mother Was Murdered.* Christ, she'd better go down to Peter and make sure that he keeps an eye on the television. It would be a disaster if one of them flicked over to a news channel.

There was no one she could think of who might recommend a psychologist, no one whom she could confide in to even search. The first number she rang took her to an answering machine. The receptionist for the second call would not put her through without first getting details of her problem. She sat back in the bed to think. Finally she was resolved that she would have to trust one of them. She rang back the second number.

"I am the person looking after the two boys whose parents were killed in Ethiopia." That was sufficient to receive a return call from Doctor Mary Horan, child psychologist. Dr. Horan listened to Denise's problem, asked for a brief period to reflect, and promised to ring her back.

Doctor Horan was herself too busy to take on the two boys. She cautioned that whatever psychologist was engaged they had to be experienced in child bereavement, and that there were few professionals with this expertise. However, she had been told of a psychologist who was setting up a practice in Ireland – the person was English, and came highly recommended. Doctor Horan had phoned the English lady and discussed the case with her. Doctor Horan was satisfied that the woman was not only suitably qualified, but she had considerable experience in the specific field of child bereavement. She was not too busy, and she had agreed to meet the guardians and, if they were happy with her, to take on the case. A mobile number was exchanged. Before Denise had left the bedroom she had spoken to Sue Hobbs, child psychologist, whose practice was in Celbridge, less than an hour from Mullingar. Sue would call to Ballyboe in the afternoon. She could be introduced as Denise's friend, but she advised that the boys would have to be subsequently told that she had met other such children who had lost their parents, and that she had been able to help them. No, they should not tell the boys that their mother was dead, not yet.

What a relief. And to think that we talked last night about simply sitting the boys down and telling them straight out.

One worry over. Now she had to brave the weather and the paparazzi to go to the chemists to buy antigen tests.

Better test everyone. No good bringing this child psychologist into a house full of Covid. So, that's the five of us, plus Tom. Might as well buy two packets of five. It'll be a disaster if all, or even some, of us have the Covid. I'd have to ring this Sue Hobbs and put her off. I wonder if she'd mind coming and sitting with us, if all of us were wearing masks? We'll see.

Omer

Omer and Tenen are in their bedroom, the door shut. Nobody is allowed in. Tenen is buried under the bedclothes, with only his hand protruding. He has been crying. Pitifully. Now he is just sobbing. His hand is in Omer's hand, the two brothers sharing their grief. Omer rubs his brother's hand, but that only sets him off crying again. Denise wants to come in, but, no, they don't want her. They just want to be alone. Denise wanted to cuddle them, but they wouldn't let her. Uncle Peter wanted to come and stay in the room with them, but they don't want him either. They don't want anyone. They can hear muffled sounds from outside the door.

Uncle Peter knocked and asked, "you boys okay in there?" But we didn't answer.

They told us, that is Uncle Peter told us, that Mama is sick. She's in hospital. Uncle Peter says she is very sick. She has the Coronavirus. In Ethiopia they don't have vaccines, so Mama didn't get the needle into her arm. And because she didn't get any vaccination she got the virus. We are very sad. First of all we were to meet Mama in Addis Ababa, and she was coming back to Ireland with us. But that didn't happen. Then they told us that she would be coming on the plane the next day. We were waiting for her. She didn't come. Now we don't know when she is coming. Why can't she just come here and we can mind her? She can get the vaccination here in Ireland.

Our granny is sick too. She's our Irish granny. We had another granny in Ethiopia, but she died. Uncle Peter said our Irish granny also has the virus. I hate this virus. Yesterday I made a drawing of a Coronavirus monster. My monster is really fierce looking. He has big teeth and horns out of his head. Denise put the picture up on the wall in the kitchen. The monster will frighten any viruses that come into the house. I think I will draw a few more Coronavirus monsters. I could give them to anyone who wants one. Maybe the old man, Tom, would like one for his house. It would scare the virus away if it came to his house.

We liked the sausages Uncle Peter fried for breakfast. He said they were Clonakilty sausages. Clonakilty sausages are our favourite sausages. I ate four of them, and Tenen ate three. The old man, he's the one who drove us from the airport, came in and he had a sausage. He's really old. He has a beard. But I think he's nice. I counted the sausages that Uncle Peter fried. There were sixteen. I got four, Tenen got three, Tom got one, Audrey got three, Denise got two and Uncle Peter got two. There was one left over, so I said we should give that to Stella. Stella didn't eat it, I mean she didn't chew on it, she just swallowed it down. Then she wanted more, but there wasn't any more.

After the breakfast Uncle Peter said that it had stopped raining. So we went outside to play football. Uncle Peter said we should only play in the lower garden. We shouldn't go out the front of the house. I don't know why. There seems to be people outside the gate. Audrey came with us. I don't like Audrey. She just wants to bully Tenen. I told her to leave him alone. If she bullies him again I'm going to give her a slap. And everywhere she goes she carries this doll with her. Audrey is no good at football. Stella was running after the ball and barking. I was throwing the ball to Tenen, but he couldn't catch it. So Stella was pouncing on the ball. She was trying to bite it, but it's too big and she can't get her teeth at it.

My friend, Tony, called to our house yesterday. He lives around the corner, on the main road. Uncle Peter called me out to wave hello to him. But he wasn't allowed in 'cause we have the Covid in the house. Uncle Peter asked Tony to come by next week when the Covid will have gone away, and he said he would. I'm really pleased about that.

When we were kicking football Denise went to the shops and she brought back these tests to see who has the virus. We never had any test before. Maybe they just didn't have them in Ethiopia. We each got a packet that we had to open. I opened Tenen's, 'cause he wasn't able to. Inside there were more packets that we had to open. Uncle Peter and Denise showed us how to do the test. We had to take this probe – it was like the buds that Mama cleans our ears with, only on a longer stick – and push it up our noses. I didn't like that. Tenen didn't either. Denise said we should shove it up and twist it. But it hurt. She said, "let me do it for you." I cried, but she said she was finished. Then it was Tenen's turn. He ran away. So, Uncle Peter had to go and get him. He roared. He screamed when Denise put the bud up his nose.

Then Denise put the probe into a very small, plastic tube with water in it. But she said it wasn't water, it was a chemical. It looked like water. Then she poured some of the chemical onto this white disk. Three drops, I think. She said that if a second line showed, then that would mean that we had the virus. We had to wait for a while. A second line came almost straight away on Uncle Peter's disk. So, he has the virus. But, I think he knew he already had the virus. We waited, but no lines showed on ours. That's no second line, 'cause there was already one line. So, we don't have the virus. But Denise told us we would have to go to the doctor and get vaccinated. The doctor will stick a needle into our arms. If we haven't the virus why do we have to be vaccinated? Old Tom, he didn't have the virus either. Or Audrey. Only Uncle Peter.

Denise cooked spaghetti for lunch. It was lovely. Then we all had ice cream. 'Cause we asked for ice cream. Tenen likes chocolate ice cream. Audrey likes strawberry ice cream, but I like all ice creams. So, I had a bowl with one scoop of chocolate, one scoop of vanilla and another scoop of strawberry.

After we had lunch a friend of Denise came. Her name is Sue. She's nice. She speaks just like Denise. She was talking to Denise and Uncle Peter for a long time. Then she came over to us. She wanted to play Monopoly with me. And she was very good at it. I didn't have to explain the game to her. She wanted to ask us lots of questions. But I just wanted to play the game. Tenen wasn't playing. He was just watching. She asked us about Papa. I said that our Papa was dead. That he died in the war. She asked us what did we think of that. I said that it was very sad, that Papa didn't want to go to the war, but they made him. She asked if that made us angry, and I said that it did. And she asked us who were we angry with. Well, we were just angry about it. I suppose we were angry with the people who made him go to war. Then we were angry with the bad soldiers who killed him. She asked us how did he die. I said he was shot. Tenen didn't talk to her at all. He just listened. Sometimes when she asked him a question he just nodded or shook his head. But he never took his fingers out of his mouth.

Helina is coming in a few days' time. The woman, Sue, asked us about Helina. I said Helina was in Ethiopia with Mama. She wanted to know if we liked Helina. I told her that we loved Helina, that she was a really nice person, and that Mama had taught her to cook Irish food.

Then Sue went away with Denise and Uncle Peter and I saw them talking in the hall. I thought she wanted to play more Monopoly, but she didn't. She stopped before the game got really going. She said she would come back soon and play with me. Denise plays Monopoly, but she's too busy. Peter has the virus and goes to lie down a lot. Anyway, Peter is not much good at Monopoly. Audrey is just all the time playing with her stupid dolls. I have nobody to play Monopoly with. But Denise promised to play a really long game with me this evening.

But I don't want to play this evening. I just want to be with Tenen. He's really sad about Mama. After Sue left Uncle Peter took us to the sofa to make us sit down. He said he had something to tell us. We didn't know what he was going to say. He said he had bad news. I don't know if the woman Sue told him the bad news. I didn't hear his phone ring. Then he told us that Mama was sick. Tenen peed in his pants when he heard that. That Audrey one pointed to the pee on the floor and said, "oh look, Tenen has peed." And she started to laugh. I was so angry with her that I nearly gave her a dig. But Tenen was crying so I had to cuddle him. I'm going to get that Audrey one. I'll ask her if she wants to play football. Then I'll give her a really hard kick on the leg. And I'll pretend that I was trying to kick the ball. I won't tell anyone. Except Tenen. He hates Audrey too.

Paul

The rituals of burying the dead in Ireland are contrastive. The nearest relatives are at once traumatised, and then harried with funeral arrangements, bereaved at the loss of a loved one, yet consoled by the number of mourners who turn up to sympathise, saturnine, and sentient of the sad occasion, yet anxious to express elation at meeting again people from their past whom they haven't seen for some time, and thanking them for taking the trouble of coming. The degree of commiseration from attendees will very much depend on the circumstances of the death of the deceased: when the death is sudden and/or tragic the mood will be subdued; if the deceased passed away after a long illness, or when the deceased was of a great age, the mood will be much more relaxed.

Ryan's Funeral Home is directly across the street from the cathedral. It is a single-storey squat building wedged between a private house on one side and the Garda Barracks on the other. Unlike other funeral homes, where local traffic jams are the norm, this one affords ample parking in the cathedral car park. The wide, glass doors are open. In its gravelled forecourt a black hearse is parked. Approximately one hundred persons are outside, some huddled into small groups, others standing alone.

The French are to the fore in handshaking. They do it every day. The only time people in Ireland greet each other with a handshake is at funerals. You shake hands with those whom you haven't met recently, but also with those you have, even your neighbours and close friends. The handshake symbolises the poignancy of the occasion.

This, the *removal*, is the first phase of the funeral arrangements. Paul Sheridan is seated beside his brother in the front row of the funeral home. They are the primary mourners. Two metres in front of them is the open coffin containing the remains of their mother. They are both dressed in sombre attire. They wear face masks, and the sign at the door recommends all who enter the room to do likewise. A steady stream of people file into the building, signing their names in the register in the hall, then joining the procession up on the left side of the seats, around to look at the body and then turning to shake hands and sympathise with the two brothers. About half of them are masked.

Some want to talk, often, to the frustration of those behind, at length, to one or both of the brothers, others simply mutter something before retreating, the commonest words are a half-whispered *sorry for your troubles.* There will be some who will sympathise just the once, either at the removal or at the funeral, but there are a remarkable number who will sympathise multiple times; at the removal, before the service, after the removal when the body is lifted into the hearse, before the funeral mass, after the funeral mass, and finally, after the actual burial itself.

At the appointed time of seven o'clock Father Dunlea sweeps into the room, his long, black, flowing robes concealing his shoes. He lifts himself up onto the small rostrum and promptly rings a bell to get the proceedings underway. That is the cue for the funeral director to politely stop the procession and usher those who haven't made it as far as the brothers into the seats.

"Thank Christ for that," Paul murmured to Peter, "me fuckin shoulder is achin from all this handshakin."

He gets a scowled look of reply from Big Brother. Okay, okay, shouldn't curse in here. But, fuck it, some people just won't let go of your hand. One big fucker just kept squeezing and shaking. I didn't even know who the fuck he was. Gimme me fuckin hand back.

Now, let's get on with this. Hope Dunlea doesn't piss about. Don't drag it out. I need a fag.

The relationship between the brothers had been until a few days ago, curt, constrained. Yeah, he was probably, no understandably, sore at me for not going to see her. I should have gone up there and told the nurses to contact me if there were any developments. But I was busy. I have a full-time job to look after. He's free to spend his day as he pleases. But the situation has changed, yeah. He has been more of a brother to me the last few days than ever before. Maybe he feels guilty about the way he's been treating me. Whatever! He's changed, for the better. I'll never forget the phonecall telling me Ma was dead. He did it so kindly.

"Paul, I have some bad news. Terrible news in fact."

I kinda knew what was coming, but I didn't say anything, waiting for the inevitable.

"Our mother passed away this morning."

"Oh shit."

"This morning at about six she finally succumbed; her heart had given up. It was a peaceful ending and I don't think she suffered in the end. I was holding her hand as the last breath left her."

"Ah, Jaysus, I should have been there as well."

"It's okay, Paul," he had said gently, "she had lost consciousness for almost twelve hours. She wouldn't have been aware of anyone near her. Don't feel in any way guilty."

This was my elder brother suddenly becoming human. It continued.

"I'm at home at the moment. I need an hour's sleep. But then I want to go back up to the nursing home. I want to thank the staff there for all they did for Mum. Would you like to come with me?"

"Sure, sure. I'd like that."

"Afterwards we'd better talk about funeral arrangements. We could go from the nursing home to Ryan's. Or maybe have a coffee somewhere."

"Okay, you just give me a call when you're ready."

How long ago is it that we acted like brothers? Why, when he picked me up we actually embraced. Not a really whole-hearted embrace, y'know, more a shoulder to each other. Then we set off, first to the nursing home and then to the undertakers. Grand little car he has. Never was in it before. Wish I could afford one. Dunno about electric, though.

Ma was in the bed. Jaysus, she looked as white as a sheet. When I saw her it hit me hard. I started sobbing. I wanted to go over and wake her up. Ma, we're here. Your sons. He put his arm around my shoulder and gave me a gentle tap on the back. That woman was a great mother. Peter was the old man's pet, but Ma had a soft spot for me. The old man would shout and fuck me, but Ma was always kind. When I was short of cash she would slip me a few notes. Unbeknownst to the old man, mind you. I didn't want to remember her when she got the Alzheimer's; I just wanted to think of her when she was normal.

Peter had a big bunch of flowers. I thought they were for the funeral, but no, they were for Nurse Radley. The nurse told us that Ma would not have had that long left, even before the virus hit. She said that old people with Alzheimer's generally didn't last more than a few years after the diagnosis. She whispered to us that there was a suspicion that the carriers of the virus into the home were the nurse and doctor who had come to administer the second booster. Ironic! Professionals who are there to protect you from the virus actually give it to you.

Peter thanked the nurse, then he made a short speech, which I thought was very humane of him. Nurse Radley was very pleased with her flowers.

Then we headed off to the undertakers. The men in black. Fuckin fleecers. God, I never thought there was such a choice of coffins. We had to browse through them.

The prices! Fuckin rip off. Them bastards get you when you are bereaved, when you're vulnerable and just want to get through the agony of it, and they quietly screw you. You don't want to appear cheapskate, given the occasion, so you don't really look at the numbers. I tell you, it wouldn't be me.

Well, I assume he's paying for everything. I haven't a bob. So far he hasn't mentioned anything. I'll just keep quiet. Wait and see what he comes up with, if anything. I'd have gone myself for the cheapest coffin. I mean, who gives a shit when it's down at the bottom of a hole. But, no, he wanted a varnished oak one. The funeral man asked us if we wanted Ma to have a face mask. He said they would stuff cotton wool, soaked in chemicals up her nose, so that there was no chance of any Covid coming out. He said these were in accordance with the HSE's recommendations. Yeah, we went along with that. We said, that is, Peter said, we wanted people to see her as she was.

Will you just listen to that bollicks Dunlea. Spoutin rubbish. You'd think he was the best friend of the family. Sure, he was hardly ever out there. And I don't know if he ever went up to the nursing home. Bet he doesn't know she had Alzheimer's. It'd be funny if he said he had a chat with Ma only a few days ago. And she away with the fairies. And there's the other fucker, Collins, only a young lad, the snot not yet dry on his nose. Always hanging onto the coattails of Dunlea. What is he, a trainee priest? And acting as if he was like a father figure, a counsellor. A young fella, half my age. He came up to me and shook my hand, expressing his sympathies. I was just about to have a fag. So, I jokingly offered him one. Oh, no, he never smoked in his life. Shocked, he was to be offered one. Then he asked what about the two boys, the orphans, he called them. I told him they were out in Ballyboe, and that they all had the Covid. Ah, fair enough, he said.

Peter

Ballyglass Cemetery, the town's premier burial site, used to be a relatively constricted park, bounded on the west by the limestone wall of the Longford Road, the area within punctuated by evergreen trees of columnar yews and cypresses. Several kilometres from the town and across the road from St. Finian's College, the graveyard was small for such a big town. It was difficult to impossible to acquire a burial site there. But then, in the eighties, more land was added, so that today the cemetery is sprawled over many hectares. Unfortunately, the Council neglected to landscape the new lands, so that there is a degree of shade and definition in the original park, but just headstone after endless headstone in the extension.

Such a dreadful pity that the Council didn't set down ground rules for the cemetery, maybe allow the Council Planning Department to vet every new plot; put some degree of control on headstones; restrict the gaudiness of installations, require some shrubs and trees to be planted. This is like a miniature Dallas, the city where you could build what you liked; planning permission not required.

Peter is wandering the park on his own. He wanted some time by himself, time to remember his mother, away from the eyes of the many who have just attended her funeral. So, after Father Dunlea had thanked the faithful for coming, Peter began to sneak away. He had not gone far before the priest caught up with him.

"Peter, Peter," the elderly man was out of breath trying to catch up, "I wanted a word."

Peter stopped. "Thank you, father, for all you've done. Your kind words were very moving."

"Ah, she was a great woman. But, sure, the good Lord felt it was time for her to join Him. And who are we to argue."

"Indeed."

"I wanted to ask you about the two boys, the orphans. What is…."

"They're slowly recovering, Father, at home from the Covid." I have to convey to him, in as polite, but as abrupt, a way as possible that I do not want to talk about the boys.

"Ah, that's what I thought. I hope they'll be alright. I'll call out to see yous all in a day or so."

"Grand." I wanted to say don't bother for a week, but that would surely prolong the discussion. Peter began to walk away. And the little priest beat a retreat, leaving Peter with a "bless you," in his wake.

The undulating lands are generally a sepulchral place. The cemetery will usually be devoid of people during the autumn, winter and spring, except on those days of a funeral. Only in the summer will there be life. That is because the Sunday of the August Bank Holiday weekend has been, for many decades, Cemetery Sunday. On that afternoon the townsfolk will descend on the graveyard to pray for the dead. Lead by the clergy there will be hundreds there to say the Rosary. Graves will have been weeded and prepared for weeks in advance, each one vying for admiration with its neighbour. When your family stand in front of their plot they don't want to be ashamed. So, if you haven't had time or you have forgotten to work on the grave, then you simply don't turn up.

Peter has never been through such a prolonged period of stress in his life. Sure, there was the time when his father died, but nothing as continuous as this. First there was the awful news of Amare's death, then Mary's, followed by the worry of rescuing the boys, the tension of getting them passed the soldiers, then through airport and safely out of Ethiopia. Throw into that the complication of this girl, Helina. Add in the virus that he picked up. Now he had to worry how to break the news to the boys that their mother was dead; the paparazzi at the gate, people – first Paul and now Father Dunlea – wanting to come and visit; unable to tell them why. And on top of all this Mum picks this time to catch the Covid and die. And the stress is scheduled to continue: Mum will be just buried when Helina will arrive; a time will have to be chosen to break the news of Mary's death to the boys; after that we will have to plan their rehabilitation into the community, school, get them vaccinated.

But he is only too appreciative of the great help that people are rendering him. Denise especially has been just wonderful. He would have been lost without her. She is so mentally strong. And so intuitive. She is simply marvellous with the boys, integrating them into what is becoming our little family, playing with them, feeding them, but most of all just listening to them. She can really come down to their level. And Audrey seems to be gelling well with them. How on earth did Denise find this woman Sue Hobbs? Very professional and tactful person.

Then there's Tom. What a friend to have when you most need it. Nothing is a bother. He did a great job on the gates. Then ferrying me to the airport and, a week later, collecting us from Cork. He has been an ideal guardsman at the gate. Now, if I had to be out there, what would I say to them? You can't come in, you can't talk to the boys, you can't even see them. Tom's solution was so simple – everyone in the house has Covid. No more was necessary. Would anyone believe that he's seventy-eight? I'll have to find a way to thank him. He likes a drop of malt, but, sure that won't be enough.

God, I'm relieved to be over this Covid. It really took a lot out of me. It started with a tickly cough; then it went into my chest; my sinuses were blocked; I found it difficult to sleep because, no matter which way I turned in the bed, my breathing was laboured; I think the blocked sinuses contributed to prolonged headaches; I felt tired and listless all the time. Well, I'm over it now, and I feel in really good form.

Mrs. Hobbs didn't take long to read our situation. She took it all in so quickly. You can't beat a professional person. No, she said, we must never tell the boys that their mother was murdered. Too tragic for their young minds. It could have the most awful long term effects on them. Dying of Covid would be less traumatic.

"I never, well, virtually never, lie to anybody, even small children. When they do find out the truth, and the likelihood is that they will, it will diminish their trust in you. But, in these circumstances, I think we have to do it."

After the tragic death of a parent they would most likely exhibit many of the characteristics of acute posttraumatic stress response, she advised. As a result the child may present as numb or mute. She diagnosed that the death of their father had not had a serious effect, but we all had to be most careful about the death of the mother. She was more concerned with Tenen than with Omer. We might expect Omer to exhibit diminished self-esteem, and he may develop a tendency to do uncharacteristic, naughty things. Both of them need to be praised for their courage in accepting their loss. The death of their grandmother from Covid should be looked upon as helpful, even though she appreciated that, for me, this was a very sad moment in my life. The children had now direct contact with a person dying from Covid, so that it may be beneficial for them to then deal with their mother dying from it. It would have been useful for the boys to go to their grandmother's funeral, to get more acquainted with death, but she recognised that was impossible because of the probability of them becoming prematurely aware that their mother was dead, even, God forbid, murdered. A more important reason for them not going to the funeral would be that they might then expect the corpse of Mary to be brought home and be buried, just as they had witnessed with their grandmother.

She suggested that we tell the boys of their mother's death when Helina arrived, not before. It would be Helina who brought the sad news with her from Ethiopia. And Helina may be an added comfort to them.

In spite of our circumstances, we gave Mum a good send-off. It was a pity we couldn't have had a traditional wake for her in the house, but the get-together in the hotel was fine and fitting. So many people turned up; cousins from England, old friends of my father's, all of Mum's bridge club, Jerome, and Margaret from next door, Tom's friends, a whole hape of them came from Westmeath County Council, the editor of the Irish Times, the four priests of the parish: sure half the town was there. And Paul behaved himself. Going around thanking people for coming, asking them if they would like another drink. If only he hadn't had a fag continually hanging off his lip.

Now I need to sit down and work on my finances. The nest egg I saved is well and truly eaten into by now. When the boys are settled I need to look at getting out and earning a crust again. The Irish Times want me to update Chile and Argentina. Maybe it's time for an article about wine tasting in Mendoza. I'll have a chat with Jerome some time.

Tom

Stella has joined Tom at the edge of his wildflower meadow. She knows that Tom will take her for a walk around the field, over to the wood. It's a regular walk they make in the mornings. It is the middle of spring and the grasses and flowers are already knee deep. Prolonged rain followed by sunshine has boosted growth. The lush meadow hums to the bees hovering from flower to flower. Yes, the presence of so much ragwort is such a pity, but, overall, the field is a joy to him. Wildlife needs fields like these. Man needs fields like these. It lifts our spirits.

On the perimeter of the field there is a distinctive path, made by foxes, as they make their way from the woodland into the farmland. He has often seen them in the late evening or early morning. Tails so oversized that Tom wonders how nature came to bestow the animals with them. What purpose do these enormous tails serve? They regularly go hunting, generally for rabbits, and Ballyboe is plentiful with the long-eared, white-tailed, little mammals. Indeed, the foxes are not the only wildlife that feed on the rabbits. There is a family of buzzards living in the wood that depend on them for food. Stella will accompany Tom into the wood, up alongside the stream, where Tom will spend time peering with his binoculars at the buzzard's nest. There is a down-covered chick in the nest and the chick will look down from it at any intruders. In about two weeks the chick will fletch. Whilst Tom is quietly monitoring nest activity Stella will drench herself in the stream.

He surveys his wildflower meadow, his corncrake field. When I was a child my father would have me watching and listening for the corncrake. They would be arriving in Ballyboe about now, and they would stay here during the summer. Sadly we haven't seen or heard a corncrake here for many decades. Mechanised grass cutting has been the problem, and the birds are now only seen on the northwest coast and neighbouring islands. But, Tom's earnest wish is that one day they may return to the Midlands. This meadow of mine would be an ideal place for them. I remember my father making the sound of a corncrake. He took two combs and rubbed one against the other. The sound he made was about right, but I could never figure out how the bird created that sound. Was it its tongue vibrating? You might often hear the corncrake, but rarely would you see one. You'd be listening and standing on high ground looking into the field, watching for the grass to move.

Tom has had an eventful morning. It started with the phone call from Kevin. The night before Tom had brought up the matter of Kevin moving in with him, but Kevin had been distinctly unenthusiastic. But the phone call was to change all of that.

"I've changed my mind," Kevin said, "I've decided it's time for me to move out of the town. So, I will happily move in with you."

"Great."

"But only on one condition."

"Yeah, what's that?"

"That we get married first."

"Well, that's a big change. Why make marriage a condition? Sure, you know I was the one who wanted that in the first place."

"I'm coming to the end, Tom. Maybe another year or two. I want to leave you whatever little bit I have. If we are married you can avoid inheritance tax. Simple as that."

"You should leave your house to your nephew. I don't need it. But, look, we'll talk about that later. Kevin, I'm on gate duty and there's a car here, blowing its horn. G'luck."

The agitated driver in the car was Father Dunlea. Now there was never any love lost between him and me, so I gave him short shift. I think I might have insulted him, well, simply told him to fuck off, and I hope Peter won't be too annoyed.

Tom hears the shouting from the Sheridan garden next door. The eldest boy is calling Stella. Stella has probably had enough of them for the moment and wants a walk and a bath. Tom calls back, "Stella is over here with me." Shortly afterwards he sees the two little heads looking over the hedge at him.

"Stella and I are going for a walk over into the wood. D'you want to come with us?"

"Yes," the eldest boy replies.

"Fine. Then I'll send a text to your uncle that the three of us are off for a walk."

Tom has to make a passage through the fuchsia hedge for the boys to get through.

"Who owns this field?" Omer asks, excitedly.

"Why, this field is mine."

But the little boy, Tenen, is obviously not happy, and he begins to return to the gap in the hedge.

"What's the matter, Tenen?" Tom asks.

"Grass is too high. Too many nettles and stingy things."

"That's alright," says Tom, "I can carry you." He reaches down and the boy accepts his hands in lifting up to his chest. The boy seems quite at ease in Tom's arms.

"I'll get out my machete and cut you guys a hole in that hedge and in the long grass, so that yous can come into my field."

"Why don't you cut this grass?" Omer enquires, "it's so long."

"I let the grass grow long for a special reason. D'you want to know why?

"Oh huh."

"This field is the corncrake field. Well, it used to be the corncrake field. But the birds left many years ago and they haven't been back, but one….."

"What's a corncuake?" Tenen interrupts.

"Corn crake," Omer corrects.

"A corncrake is a bird about the size of a pigeon, but not as fat as a pigeon. It's speckled brown in colour and it has a rather long skinny neck."

"But," Omer is confused, "I still don't see why the grass is so long."

"Ah, well, the corncrake is a very shy and secretive bird. It doesn't like to be out in the open. It prefers to wander around in the long grass. And it makes its nest in the long grass."

"I never saw a corncuake," Tenen announces.

"Corn crake," Omer corrects again, loudly this time.

Tom sets Tenen down and tells them all about corncrakes, the rasping sound they make, how he used to watch and listen for them when he was a child, why the birds no longer come because the grass cutters kill their chicks, and of his earnest wish that they would one day return to his field.

"So, if people stopped cutting the grass," Omer was circumspecting, "then the chicks wouldn't get killed, and the birds would live here with their family."

"Exactly. However, farmers need to have grass to feed the cows in the winter."

"Oh, yeah." Omer is pensive. "Okay," he has a solution, "let's say that every second field is for birds, and the others are for the cows."

"That's a very good suggestion."

Father Patrick Dunlea

Yesterday Father Dunlea attended the diocesan meeting, an emergency session called by the bishop to deal with administration. The diocese of Meath has over one hundred priests who are assigned to the diocese's sixty-nine parishes. Covid has wreaked havoc. So many priests are down with it that it has become necessary to deploy the healthy ones to cover the work of others. The bishop wanted Father Collins to be moved temporarily to Enfield, leaving Mullingar with just Dunlea and his two African priests.

I felt I couldn't just come out and say to his excellency that Father Collins would not be capable, even for a few days, of assuming the role of parish priest. The lad is not the full shilling. He wouldn't be able to cope. He'd be lost. But the bishop seems to think that Collins is fine, so off he went. Now I'm left with these two blacks that my flock, I fear, are very uncomfortable with. They're grand lads, and they know their stuff, but I'll have to spoon-feed them.

The Sheridans. Father Dunlea has had a particular interest in the Sheridans because they were always seen as a stalwart family in the town. Jim Sheridan was a member of the parish council for many years before his demise. Indeed, as far as Father Dunlea remembers, he was one of the founding members of Mullingar Parish Council. And his wife, can't remember her name, was it Anne, sure I buried her not so long ago, she was the flower person, deciding on what flowers should be put on the altar. He had been encouraging Peter to join the council, and he had served on it for a brief period, but he said he was too busy with his work, he was away writing about foreign travel so much. Pity. He's such a sound fellow; well-educated and articulate, not like some of those who I'd like to get rid of. But we just couldn't hang on to him. And now I'm afraid that his faith is under attack; they tell me he has a relationship with some married English woman, a woman with a child, and one who does not attend our church. Fornicating with a non-believer, or, worse still, maybe with a Protestant!

Father Dunlea's interest in the Sheridans was heightened when the bishop took him aside after the diocesan meeting.

"What's the latest on these two orphans in Mullingar? Y'know the sons of the murdered woman. It's all over the news. Wasn't the mother one of the Sheridans of Mullingar, the daughter of Jim Sheridan, that man whom I met at a parish council meeting?"

Dunlea was rather speechless. Yes, the boys were grandchildren of Jim Sheridan, but he didn't know any more than people would read in the papers. Their mother, can't remember if she was Anne or Mary, no, Anne was the mother, Jim's wife. Must be Mary, then. Anyway, the daughter certainly grew up in the faith, but, then she was gone, off living in Dublin. I never noticed her again in the cathedral. Even when she'd be home. The papers say she married a black man from Ethiopia. Most of the people in Ethiopia, as far as I know, are Christians, slightly different faith to ours. Well, if the bishop has an interest, then I'll have to make it my business to find out. So, hopefully, I can get back to his excellency with a report. Maybe even a favourable report; that the boys had been baptised; that they were being brought up as Catholics; that they were coming to church with their uncle. I mentioned to Peter after the funeral that I'd pop out to them. They should be over the Covid by now. Dump-didily-ump-bump-bum-bum.

When he goes visiting, Father Dunlea never announces, or arranges anything; he simply turns up, and, sure, God is good, and things always work out. But that wasn't the case when he arrived at the Sheridan house in Ballyboe.

The damn gates were locked. A hefty padlock. No bell or anything to ring. He tried rattling the gates.

"Hello!" No response. But he thought he heard a faint voice coming from the garden. He returned to his car and blew the horn.

"Yes?" an elderly voice presently enquired. He couldn't see who it was. It certainly wasn't Peter. The gates had vertical timbers fixed to them on each side of the frame, so you had to peer sideways to see in.

"Who's that?" Dunlea asked.

"The gate man," came the reply. Dunlea caught a glimpse of the bearded man through the timbers. He knew this man. Draper. A homosexual. Notorious. Lives here in Ballyboe. Known to the Guards.

"Will you open the gates, please." Firm but polite.

"No, I won't. Nobody is allowed to come in."

"Do you know who I am?"

"Oh, ho, I know you alright. You're the priest. You're the one who came one day with the Guards, accusing me of horrible things. You're one of those holding up the liberal march of the Irish people. Oh, I remember hearing about your speeches from the pulpit. Yeah, first you opposed divorce, then abortion, and I suppose you were also against gay marriage. Oh, I know you alright."

What a thing to say to me! No respect at all for the cloth. What is the world coming to?

"How dare you speak to me like that, you heathen, you…you… abuser of children. How dare you. Now, go and call Peter Sheridan. I want to talk to him."

"Abuser of children? Yous men of the cloth are the abusers, the paedophiles."

"Enough of this. Call Mr. Sheridan."

"He's lying down. Asleep."

"I don't care what he's doing. Get him up. I insist that you call him." Father Dunlea's face was red and his pulse was racing.

"And I insist that you get in your car and fuck off." Tom Draper's pulse was going faster.

Father Dunlea had no option but to beat a retreat. If he had his mobile phone with him he might have been able to use it. So he drove back to the parochial house. He was fuming. That filthy homosexual. Twenty years ago there were none of them in Catholic Ireland. Now, they are appearing and multiplying. We even had one of them as our Taoiseach! Can you imagine. LGBTs, Pride. In Catholic Ireland! Wait 'til I meet Peter. I'll tell him how I was treated. At his own gate.

It was Missus Simmonds who found the number and made the call. Father Dunlea couldn't understand why Peter didn't want him to come back to Ballyboe, preferring that Peter would come to him. But I wanted to see the two boys. What's the problem? No, Peter would come to the parochial house in the morning.

Mrs. Simmonds served them tea in the front parlour.

"Now, Peter, I first want to tell you about that neighbour of yours. That queer. He was most insulting. Not only would he not let me in the gate, but he had the common cheek to tell me to f off. Me, the parish priest, being blasphemed at. I can tell you I was shocked. Shocked. To be treated like that. At your own gate."

"I'm very sorry about that, Father. I'll speak to him about it."

"Speak to him!" Father Dunlea's voice was raised. "I should think you'd do more than that."

"Father, we've all been under a lot of pressure. The reporters at the gate, lots of people wanting to come in....

"Peter, I'm not just a common person. I'm the parish priest."

"I know, Father, I know."

"Now." Dunlea needed to press on. "What about these boys of yours?"

"Well, Father, we have a difficulty."

"What difficulty?"

"You see, I have to look out for the mental state of mind of the boys. They've lost their father first, and then their mother….."

"Yes, yes, I'm quite aware of the situation. But, Peter, surely you should be thinking of their souls first, not just their state of mind. Those boys need to be nurtured under the guidance and love of God and His holy church."

There was a prolonged pause in the conversation. Peter reached for his cup of tea, but he seemed to be composing himself.

"Is there something I'm not understanding, Peter."

"Yes, I'm afraid there is, Father."

"Go on."

"We are acting under the guidance of a child psychologist."

"I see. And what, pray, does that have to do with the matter?"

"She advises us to keep the boys isolated for the time being."

"Fair enough. Keep them isolated. But not from the church and their God."

"There's one of the delicate matters that we have," Peter began, "the boys have not been brought up Catholics, indeed, not Christian…."

"But I thought the Ethiopians were all Christians."

"No, you see, Father, Mary and her husband were non-believers. Atheists."

"Atheists! Oh, dear God." Dunlea was distraught. How was he going to relate this to the bishop. He thought for a while, looking sideways at Peter. Then he spoke, calmly and consolingly.

"Peter, God had seen fit to entrust you with the care of them boys. You, and you alone, are their guardian. It should be your mission to correct the boys' past and bring them into the fold. They're young and it's early in their mental development. It's up to you to ensure that they receive a proper education. Do you see what I mean?"

"Father, my sister, Mary, and her husband didn't want their boys to be brought up with any particular religious beliefs. They…."

Once again, Father Dunlea interrupted. "But, they're dead, man. And you have the mantle now. Grasp it. Bring them to the Church next Sunday and we'll have them baptised."

Peter finally dropped his submissiveness and spoke forcibly. "No, Father. I'm resolved to leave the matter of religion for the time being. Maybe in the future, when the boys have gotten over the terrible tragedy of their parents' deaths, I will tell them about God."

"Maybe! Maybe in the future! Peter, oh, Peter, I can't believe this is coming from you."

Peter stood up to leave. It seemed that he didn't want to say anything else.

"Let me ask you one thing," Father Dunlea implored, "if his grace, Bishop Clohessy, was free, would you agree to meet him? To explain your predicament."

"No, Father. I won't meet anyone. Not now. Not in the immediate future. I have to get the boys settled first. Thank you for seeing me and thank Mrs Simmonds for the tea." And with that he was gone.

Denise

It is early afternoon in Ballyboe. Denise is clearing the plates and washing dishes, looking out the kitchen window. The house is relatively quiet. Peter has gone to the airport to collect Helina. Sue Hobbs is on the floor of the living room playing Monopoly with Omer. Audrey is sitting at the table, colouring in a drawing she made. Tenen is watching her, his two fingers stuck in his mouth, his little lamb under his arm. Denise can see Tom Draper weeding around the shrubs in the drive, availing of the dry weather. The gate is locked, but there is nobody outside it. The reporters have given up waiting there. The story of the murdered mother and her children is gone from the papers – history - and other news' stories have replaced it.

Sue has an innate fear of dogs, that I find intriguing. She's just scared of dogs, any dog. You consider a child psychologist, a person trained to see, analyse and understand the logic of life, the things that should matter, and the things that shouldn't. Outwardly you wouldn't find a more logical and practical person. So, her fear of dogs, particularly friendly ones like Stella, is contradictory. I remember the first morning she arrived. Of course, Stella barked, yes, pretty loudly, after all it was a new machine in his territory. Sue just sat in her car. We were waiting for her to emerge, but all she did was open the window.

"The dog," she said, "could you take the dog away."

Well, we ushered Stella to her bed, thinking little of it. But then anytime the dog appeared Sue was petrified. I tried to explain that Stella is the gentlest creature you could meet, but she wouldn't have it.

"No dog, however placid it appears, can be trusted. Especially around children."

And her fear was reinforced when Stella, obviously aware of her fear and/or contempt for him, barked her back into her car. The next time she visited, when we had a chance to chat, she told me that, when she was a child, the so-called friendly dog from next door attacked her and would have savaged her had it not been for the intervention of its owner. Ever since then her fear of dogs has not diminished. So, every time Sue is coming we have to get Stella and order her into her box.

Audrey has eaten very little of the lunch that was laid out. Denise had decided that it was high time she stopped preparing special meals for her, that the girl would either eat what everyone else was eating, or she would go hungry. But, so far it hasn't worked. Omer and Tenen are great eaters. Salads, even tomatoes, spicey foods, fruits, any kind of meat, nothing is any problem for them. Maybe it was because of the awful food they had to eat in Ethiopia. It was amusing watching little Tenen stuffing the lettuce into his mouth, leaf after leaf. But the list that Audrey refuses to eat is getting longer. She won't eat mushrooms, fish, pepper salami, any kind of strong cheese, even bread with seeds in it. They had pizzas last night and Audrey picked out all of the little pieces of mushroom before she put a morsel in her mouth. When it comes to meals Omer seems to be always distracted. Inevitably, he finds something else of interest just when the meal is on the table. Although everyone else is tucking in, he is in another world. You can command him to eat a hundred times, but his little mind is elsewhere. So, Denise simply forks it into his mouth. And he seems oblivious to it, mechanically opening when the spoon is close to his lips. Then, all of a sudden, he picks up his fork and gobbles what's left in a few seconds.

After the pizzas there was a special treat for everyone. Peter had brought back a selection of cakes from the bakery. Each cake was generous in size. Omer said he wanted the apple strudel. Peter was about to cut the cake in half, when Omer said he wanted all of it.

"I want some of it as well," Audrey interjected.

"You can have the strawberry cake," Omer dismissed her.

"No, I want apple strudel."

"Okay," Peter said, watching Omer grabbing the cake. "But you won't be able to eat all of it, and when you are full, we will divide the rest of it." The apple strudel was enormous, an adult meal in itself.

"I will eat all of it," Omer said defiantly.

"Bet you won't," Audrey challenged, her arms folded in front of her.

"I bet you five euros you won't be able to eat all that apple strudel," Peter said. "Why, even I couldn't eat it all."

"So, if I eat it all, I get five euros?"

"Yes, but you have to eat every crumb," Peter said with a smile. "If you drop a crumb on the floor, then it doesn't count. You have to eat every single crumb. And if you are not able to eat it all, you have to give me five euros."

"O.K."

The four of them watched as Omer began his quest. It seemed at times that he had put too much into his mouth, that it would get stuck in his throat and he would have to vomit it. But the lad steadily devoured the entire apple strudel. He never looked up once, and he was careful not to let a single crumb escape. Peter and Denise tentatively clapped, but were afraid the cake might all suddenly get vomited back. Then Peter reached into his back pocket and gave Omer his prize.

"You won your bet," he said. "Well done."

"What are you going to bet me?" Audrey asked.

"And me," chirped Tenen.

"Okay, let's see," Peter began to think, "next time we are eating, say, breakfast, you, Audrey, have to eat everything on your plate, okay?"

"Okay," said a smiling Audrey, "but it has to be sausages, or rashers....or a boiled egg."

"No, no," Omer protested, "whatever is on the plate. You can't just say what."

"But you just ate something you like," Audrey argued.

"And me?" little Tenen asked.

"You," Peter began, "let's see. Suppose we say that I will bet you five euros if you don't suck your fingers from now until you go to bed."

Tenen thought for moment and, getting out of his seat, said, "no, I'm not betting that." And all the others laughed.

Harmony between the three children did not always prevail. There were regular fights, particularly between Omer and Audrey. Yesterday morning Audrey came in bawling pitifully.

"What's the matter," Denise asked, taking Audrey and cuddling her.

"Omer kicked me on the leg," she cried.

In these disputes the natural tendency was for Denise to see the matter from Audrey's side. This, after all, was her little girl, her baby, whom she loved more than anything else in the world. And her little angel would never do anything wrong. Any such row had to be the other party's fault. However, she had being cautioning herself more and more, that she had to be impartial, that if she always took her daughter's side then Omer would never see her as a potential mother. And anything that Omer thought, you could bet that Tenen would form the same opinion. It seemed to her that Peter did not have a similar, neutral inclination. He, in Denise's opinion, always took the side of Omer, or, if it was a row between Tenen and Audrey, he sided with Tenen. She would have to talk this out with him.

"Oh, dear," Denise said, looking at Audrey's leg, "that's a nasty mark there. But I'm sure it was an accident," Denise consoled, rubbing Audrey's head tenderly.

Audrey momentarily ceased her loud sobbing to move out of her mother's arms and roar, "no, he did it deliberately. We were running after the ball, and he kicked me really hard. And I was doing nothing."

"What's wrong?" Peter appeared on the scene.

"Oh, it's Omer and Audrey again," Denise said.

Peter bent down beside the sobbing Audrey. "What did he do to you?" he asked.

"He kicked me really hard on the leg," cried Audrey, pointing to the mark just above her ankle.

"I'll go and get him," Peter said sternly, heading out the door. He came back later to say that Omer could not be found. He was hiding somewhere. "He will have to say he's sorry when he comes in," Peter assured Audrey, "or he will go to his room with no dinner."

Although Tenen was only half the size of the other two, he was well able to fight his corner. If Omer gave him a clip he would follow him, brandishing his teeth, until he got him. He would be threatening to sink his teeth into some part, any part, of Omer when Peter's voice would sound.

"Now, now, no biting. Remember what I told you about biting."

Often there is a fight between two or even the three of them. But, no matter who is not talking to whom, they are all talking to the dog. Stella is a dear. And she's so gentle and imperturbable. I see Tenen giving her little pieces of food, and the dog is so careful with him, gently taking the food off his hand or out of his little fingers. Stella loves to play with them, loves for them to chase her around the garden. If somebody picks up Stella's towel the dog will latch on to it with her teeth, and, no matter what they do, she won't let go. Stella and Tom get on very well too. If the children are inside and Tom is working in the garden, Stella will be with him, following him every step.

During the day the boys are here on their own, while Audrey is at school. All that will change in a few weeks when the schools close. Most mornings the boys tell me that they are going through the ditch into Tom's garden, where, they tell me that Tom takes them and Stella through the fields to the wood. Omer asked me the other day about corncrakes, but I told him that we don't have them anymore.

"Oh, no," he told me, "Tom has a field, the field with the long grass, and one day he says the corncrakes will come there."

I Googled corncrakes and they were very interested in seeing the pictures and reading about them.

"There is very little chance of corncrakes returning to the midlands of Ireland," I told them, "they only come to remote parts of the west of Ireland."

"But they might come back. One day." Omer was not giving up on Tom's dream.

"I don't see what's so special about corncrakes," Audrey said, "I mean, we've got lots of other birds."

Some days the boy from around the corner, Tony, comes and kicks football with Omer. They seem to get along fine with each other. Tony is a very quiet boy, unlike Omer, so Omer tends to dominate him.

Things are beginning to work out well here. We have established routines. Peter gets the breakfasts, I get the lunch, then we take it in turns to get the dinner. Peter wants to do his part, but, I will have to wean him off fries. Fried sausages, fried eggs, fried rashers, fried black pudding. Maybe I should do breakfast. Then we could have muesli, fruit salad, yoghurts, an occasional boiled egg. Even for the dinners Peter cooks there is a leaning towards using the frying pan again. And the deep-fat frier. I have to get rid of that thing out of the house. Steak and chips, lamb chops and chips, gammon steaks and chips. Oh, the kids love it, but it's not healthy for them. They'll get fat, like Paul's children. Peter really doesn't go in for fresh vegetables. What appears on the plate are either tinned or frozen.

The boys have been talking about potato cakes. Apparently their mother made them regularly in Ethiopia. I have no idea what a potato cake is. Peter says they are made from boiled potatoes, but he has never made them. Funny enough, the boys said they got potato cakes in Tom's house. I must ask him to show us how to make them.

Our evening routine is great. Whoever gets the dinner does the washing up, and the other takes the kids to bed.

There is a difficulty with that. It's not getting them to brush their teeth, or putting on their pyjamas, or getting them into the bed. It's the story. Omer wants stories of fantasy, knights fighting dragons, magic spells, thrillers. Audrey's passions are animal stories, maybe how some little rabbit got lost and eventually found its way home. Nothing too excitable. Tenen is not so particular. He will listen to anything. But, very soon after the story starts Tenen's eyes get heavy, and before the story is finished he is fast asleep. So, our routine is that the choice of story rotates between the three of them: Omer tonight; Audrey the night after; Tenen the third night. Omer has been sweet-talking Tenen, when it his turn, to choose thrillers, but Audrey has become aware of this, and she has her own persuasive ways with Tenen.

"Would you like to play house with me in the morning, Tenen? You can have two of the dolls."

The little guy nods.

"Which story are you going to pick tonight, Tenen? It's your turn. I really like the one about the little puffling, don't you?"

I don't know what it is about Monopoly, but every time anyone plays with Omer he always wins. Within half an hour of the start he has accumulated streets and houses on them, so that anyone unfortunate to land there has to pay him rent. And he's so miserly in the game. I swear, one day, that boy will be a successful businessman, a developer. Tenen is not interested in Monopoly. Audrey plays, but she never wins with Omer. Audrey's art work gets better by the day. She produces stunning, colourful displays. And her interest in painting is rubbing off on Tenen, who sits with her at the table, trying to emulate what she does.

When the kids are safely in bed Peter and I find time to relax over a glass of wine. We share stories about what the kids have been up to during the day. It's great. Last night we talked about education and religion. I related how I had to choose between a religious school for Audrey or a Gaelscoil, an Irish-speaking school. I chose the latter. I know Peter would have gone for the former. I think, rather I hope, he sees my point that Mary and Amare set out to bring up Omer and Tenen as atheists, and that to begin teaching them religion now would only confuse them. Mary and Amare told them there was no such thing as a God. If Peter is to contradict that, there is the probability of a negative reaction. Peter is still a staunch Catholic, I see that. And I see his dilemma. The parish priest now wants to interfere. Peter went to see him this morning, and, by all accounts, they had a rather terse discussion. But, Peter reported that he had resisted the priest's appeal for the boys to be brought into the church. I'm very happy about that. I just hope that he won't change his mind. Or have it changed for him. In any case, I wonder how the boys will view their new guardian believing in God.

I can now quite confidently confirm that my man, Peter Sheridan, is heterosexual. Absolutely sure, I am. Tom Draper is, and always has been, a dear friend, nothing more. Peter left me in no doubt when I asked him, point blank.

"Me and Tom?" He started to laugh. "You didn't think….did you?"

"Well, let's say I had a slight suspicion."

"Not at all. Tom is just a lovely man. A genuine, nice fellow. It never bothered me in the least that Tom had a different orientation to others. In fact, I thought it was lovely. You haven't met his future husband, Kevin, yet, but Tom and Kevin have been lovers for decades. I wouldn't warm to Kevin as much as I do to Tom, mind you, but they are a very loving couple. We'll invite them for dinner some day."

The other night Peter told me that I was the first person whom he really had sex with. Can you imagine, forty-three years old and his previous encounters have never, he said, been meaningful. He told me that, with all the others he felt awkward, inexperienced. He had no confidence as to what part of the female body he could safely touch. Oh, I showed him alright. Taught him how to excite me. But when I asked him how could I do the same for him, I just couldn't get him to open up. Too much for Peter. Can't really discuss such things. But, we'll work again on that one. I can tell you, I don't require much schooling. When I look back at our first adventures into sex, well, we, or rather Peter, has come a long way. Let's see, the first night we just went to dinner and he walked me home. Nothing more. Not even a kiss goodnight. The second time we went to the cinema – can't remember what we saw – and we came back to my place. I said I wanted to play him some music. Well, we had been talking about music that evening. We had a glass of wine and I put on something – it might have been Mozart, I can't remember. The music came to a waltzing part, and I said we could dance to that. So, I got him up, and it was the first time we touched. We did a few turns – he's not a good dancer – and then I lay into him, put my arms tight around him and touched the back of his neck. Of course he recoiled a little, but I was on a mission. Well, every stage of the process he had to led, had to be coaxed. It was completely the opposite to what normally occurs in girl-boy relationships. I'll say one thing for him, though, he's a good kisser. But that's about all.

Helina

The young lady who emerged through the Arrivals' door of Dublin airport was a stark contrast to the ragged girl who had travelled in pauper clothes through Ethiopia with Omer and Tenen. Helina was dressed in a full-length, gaily coloured dress. Her hair was tied in a bun above her head, a white ribbon dangling from it. She had on fresh lipstick, her eye-lids sported a dark blue shadow, and the perimeters had been traced out faintly in black. A very light covering of powder had been applied to her cheeks. She carried a large, new leather bag.

When she saw Peter she was sure that he would not recognise her, and she was right. She had to walk right up to him and say hello before he realised it was her.

"Oh! My," Peter said, "what a beautiful young woman you are."

This is what I hoped would happen. I wanted him to see me for what I really am. Not a poor, uneducated peasant, but a woman whom he might want to marry. I went to give him a hug, but he seemed like he wanted to go. He just picked up my bag and said that I should follow him. That was a pity.

I will never tell anyone how I was changed, where I got these clothes and my big leather bag, and the times I had in a beauty parlour, learning how to put on make-up. I will never tell anyone about it. It was the German. When Peter and his boys went away, I was on my own. Hashim wanted to go back to his job which is twenty kilometres from the city. I had no money, and I was alone in Addis. I couldn't afford to get a passport. Luckily, I am not yet nineteen, so the cost was just over sixteen hundred birr, otherwise it would have been much more. Jurgen, that's the name of the German, he said he would pay for the passport, and he made my application. He took me to a big shopping centre where I got my photograph taken. Then he bought me clothes. I knew I would have to pay him back, to reward him for his kindness, and I knew how. Peter had asked Jurgen to help me get to Ireland. I suspected, the way Jurgen was looking at me, that he desired me. Men are easy to read. My choice was very simple: forget about going to Ireland, and go back to Lalibela, or give myself to Jurgen. There was no other alternative. And I wasn't entirely sure then that this would be what Jurgen wanted.

When we came back to his hotel he said I could change in his bathroom. I showered and made myself ready for him. He sat outside on the bed. When I came out, with the new dress not buttoned up, I could see he was very nervous. I think he expected that he would have to, what is the word in English, woo me. But I went straight to him. He was panting. I was hoping he wouldn't have a heart attack. He is not a very handsome man, and he is much older than Peter. He has a fat belly, and he always has his glasses on. But, he was very gentle with me.

No, this is not the first time I have been with a man. There was a boy in Lalibela. Inati guessed that this boy wanted to touch me. She warned me about being with boys, and I know what to do so that I won't get pregnant. She got me this diaphragm that I always have with me. If I had stayed in Lalibela maybe I would have married that boy. His name was Nebab. He was nice, but his family were poor, like mine. We had to say goodbye to each other when he joined the army. Maybe he is dead now.

I know that Jurgen enjoyed my body, and I was glad I pleased him. I stayed with him in his hotel for many days, until my passport came. We ate our meals together, but always in his room. And after breakfast he took me into the city. He said that I shouldn't be in the room in the mornings, because the hotel maid mustn't see me.

He liked to buy me things. He has plenty of money. We were one day in the shopping centre when we passed the beauty saloon. I asked him if he would take me in there. And that is how I was teached to put on make-up and do my hair. Jurgen said he was very happy to see me made up, that I then looked like a western lady. He bought me this leather bag. And he helped me to buy presents for Peter and the boys in Ireland.

I bought Ethiopian spices, berbere, shiro and mitmita. Ethiopia, Jurgen said, is famous for its spices. I also bought a bottle of honey wine. We call it tej. Jurgen picked a bottle of red wine, because he said that Peter really liked the wines of Ethiopia. It's a Rift Valley wine. Jurgen said that Ethiopia makes very good wines, but nobody in Ethiopia drinks them. For the boys I got each of them a necklace, with their names cut out in Amharic on the necklace. I hope they will be pleased with them.

Peter's car is really lovely. It's so quiet. I was never in an electric car before. It was plugged in with a long cable into a box in the airport car park.

On the way from the airport Peter talked to me a lot. He told me about this city of Mullingar and about the people there. Then he told me that the boys have not yet been told that their mother, Mary, is dead. He said I should say that Mary was very sick with the virus and that she died in the hospital in Addis. I should say that Mary was supposed to come to Ireland with me, and I had been waiting for her, but she got sicker and then died. He said that it would be too traumatic for the boys to be told that their mother was killed by soldiers.

I can't believe how green Ireland is. Green grass, lots of green trees. Ireland is so much prettier than Ethiopia. Lots of rivers. No dust, like back home. And so many cars on the road. All the people here must be rich.

Peter's house is enormous. There are many rooms. And not just one bathroom, but three. And the house has a very big garden. An old man with a beard opened the gate for us. I suppose he works for Peter. The boys came running to greet me. I surely missed them, and I know that they missed me. We hugged and kissed, and they were hanging on to me then all the time. I really love those two boys. I was expecting that the boys would be waiting for me to come with their mother, and that they would ask where Mary was. But they didn't say anything.

There is a dog here, a brown dog that they call Stella. Stella was barking. I think she was also very excited. She's a lovely friendly dog. We don't have dogs like Stella in Lalibela.

But inside the house I was very puzzled. There are two women here. They seem to live in the house. One of them is name Denise and the other is name Sue. I don't know if these are Peter's wives or his sisters. I hope they are his sisters. I will have to ask Omer about them. The woman, Denise, has a little girl. I think her name is Audrey. She's very quiet and shy. I guess she is the same age as Omer.

We were only in the house a few minutes when Peter called the boys over to him. But the boys wanted to show me around the house. Peter took them by the hand and sat on the sofa. I sat beside him. Denise asked her little girl to go and play in her room.

"Boys," Peter said, "there is bad news, very bad news."

The boys were not really listening to him. They wanted to take me with them around the house. But the woman, Denise, told them to stay and listen to Peter.

"The very bad news," Peter told them, "is that your Mama is not coming." That made the boys stop and look at him. Then they looked at me. But they said nothing.

"Your Mama has died," he said. Still the boys just looked. I could tell they didn't know what is happening.

"She died yesterday of the virus," Peter continued.

It was terrible. Omer looked at Tenen and then Tenen began to cry. Omer put his arms around his brother, and then they both cried. Everybody wanted to put their arms around them, but they didn't want that. They just buried themselves on the sofa, roaring. The tears came out of my eyes and down my cheeks. I think everyone in the room, except the woman, Sue, was crying. It was just awful. The woman, Sue, was giving advice. She said we all needed to grieve, to cry out, not to hold anything back.

The crying went on for hours. The little girl came into the room and asked what was the matter, and her mother took her away. After a while the boys came to me and cried against me, and I put my arms around them and I rubbed them on the back.

The whole thing was very, very sad, but myself, I am really peaceful now that I don't have to lie to them anymore. And maybe now I can become their new mother.

We spent a very sad day in the house. Everybody was trying to be normal, but, all the time they were looking at the boys. When I asked them to show me around the house and garden, they didn't want to. But Audrey took me and showed me. And later Tenen, then Omer, came.

This morning, because it was Sunday, Peter asked me if I wanted to go to mass. I thought we might all be going to go to the church, but, no, there was only Peter and me. I already knew that Omer and Tenen didn't go to church, but I thought they might be going here in Ireland. Because Peter already told me that he went to church. So, that means that Denise and her little girl might not believe in God. It seems that many peoples in Ireland don't believe in God.

When we went off in his car he said to me thanks for what I did. And he wanted me to tell him that I would never, ever, tell the boys the true story of their mother. Of course I said yes.

The church here in Mullingar is the biggest church I have ever seen. We don't have anything as big as that in Lalibela. I'm sure we don't have anything as big as that in Ethiopia. This Mullingar must be a city as big as Addis Ababa. We were nearly late going in to the mass, and there was many people outside the big front doors, talking and smoking.

Many peoples were looking at me. They must have been wondering who I was. We met a woman who Peter said was a neighbour. I can't remember her name. I found it very difficult to understand what she was saying, but I just smiled and said yes to everything. When the priest came out, Peter seemed to be frightened of him and he took my hand and we went very fast to the car.

Peter

Studies have shown that the loss of a mother to a child was an etiological factor in the subsequent development of mental illness in adulthood.

What the hell is *etiological*? Oh, I know, this is an American paper. It's *aetiological*, meaning cause of a disease. Not a very appropriate word, is it?

Studies link childhood bereavement and suicide in adult life.

Children often assess themselves more negatively and can interpret a parent's death as desertion because they did not love them enough, and may believe they are not loveable.

Bereaved children have been known to, consciously or subconsciously, seek the answers to three questions: did I cause the death?; will it happen to me?; who will take care of me now?

Peter was sitting at the kitchen table, reading passages from the paper that Sue Hobbs had left them. Sue was now a regular visitor to Ballyboe, and Denise and he had sat through several counselling sessions with her.

Before giving us the paper Sue had cautioned that there were trends in the subsequent lives of bereaved children, but we mustn't assume that those trends would necessarily befall our two. What she said to us last night was succinct. I can tell you, it hit me fair and square and knocked me over. I'll never forget the conversation.

"The future mental stability of the boys in now in our…..when I say *our* or *we* I mean you two, with me in the background offering advice……the future mental stability of the boys depends now on you guys."

Ms. Hobbs often used the terms *you guys*.

She continued, "what the boys urgently require now is substitution. They have a large hole in their lives with the loss of their parents. You guys have to fill that hole. You have to give them family stability. Now, forgive me for being frank here, but I'm not sure if you guys are totally committed to each other…yet….would that reflect the situation?"

Denise looked at Peter and he at her.

Well, that is something we are working on. Not appropriate to confirm anything for the moment. Let's just hear all Sue has to say first.

"Okay," Sue proceeded, "let me spell it out for you. The boys need a substitute mother. You, Denise. They need a substitute father. You, Peter…."

"Wow," Peter muttered.

"Sorry, Peter. Is this something you're not comfortable with?" Sue asked.

"No, no….it's just that….well, when you put it square like that….well…..a father! I wouldn't actually be a father, would I? Rather a *guardian*. Sorry for interrupting. Just continue."

"No, Peter, you would have to fulfil the role of *substitute father*. Yes, you would be their guardian, but they need a father figure. Whether you formally go through the process of adopting them in the future is another matter. I'm talking about the here and now."

"Okay. Gotcha. Substitute father."

"It's not quite essential, but it would be important, that the substitutes both live together happily. Okay, let me park that for you to reflect on later."

"They need a permanent home." Sue proceeded. "This house is ideal. Having your little girl here is most beneficial. She can become their new sister. And this girl, Helina, will also provide a degree of security, a sense of place, and a link to their lost parents. I can't emphasise enough to you the benefit of the presence of the dog in the house. Even though I myself am frightened of them. I can see how the children love the dog. Wonderful for the boys…..and everyone else, I'd say. But they also need permanency in their substitute family. I'm not insisting – well, I can't, can I - that you guys commit to each other, but to commit to the boys."

For me, the words were gradually sinking in. I could see the significance of what Sue was saying. I looked at Denise, and she smiled back at me. I got the distinct impression that this was not something new to her, that she had already come to the conclusions being spelt out.

Sue told us that we were fortunate that we had told the boys that their mother died of the virus – that the virus happened to be around at the time – because violent death of a parent was a totally different kettle of fish to some kind of a normal death. She stressed that no one should be allowed to contradict that. That nobody would come out with the word *murder* in casual conversation. The father had died in the war. That, to the boys, was a step away from a violent death. The war was there; people died in it; Amare was unfortunately one of them. The death of my mother only a week before they were told of their mother's death, was also a beneficial occurrence, because they had experienced another person, whom they knew, dying.

I had been worried about our finances, what with neither of us working, having to support the boys, and now having a refugee in the house. And that was not to mention paying Ms Hobbs for her services. Services, I might add, that we just could not have done without. But, when I brought it up, Sue put our minds at ease.

"If you agree," she said, "I will approach the Social Services on your behalf. As I told you, I already made contact with them to introduce myself and inform them that I am dealing with the case. I would be very confident, from that initial conversation, that they will be sympathetic and well-disposed to your financial predicament. After all, if the boys had returned to Ireland as orphans, with nobody to look after them, the Social Services would have had to find and pay for foster parents; they would have had to pay my fees, and now, with an Ethiopian refugee in the house, well, they would have funded that as well."

"That would be great," Peter said.

"Whilst I'm at it," she continued, "I will mention the expenses you incurred in going to Ethiopia and bringing them back. Now, you won't get rich on what you get from the Irish Social Services, but at least you will have the funds to soldier on with what you are doing."

"I suppose I'd better move my stuff out of the house in town," Denise said, "and move in here. Then I don't have to pay the rent there."

There were searching looks from each of them to the others.

"From my point of view," Sue advised, "you having another house somewhere else is a negative factor. The boys need to be assured that you are here, and that there is no possibility of you going, or staying anywhere else."

Once again, Denise looked at Peter and he at her.

"The Social Services will want to know our long term plans for the boys. I mean, legal plans."

"How do you mean," Peter asked.

"Well, as we touched on just now, at the moment they are orphans, being cared for by their uncle, as their guardian, and his ....friend or partner. They will want to know if there are any proposals to formally adopt the boys."

"We need to talk," Denise said.

"Fine," said Sue as she got up to put her coat on.

"Ehh...before you go," Denise started, "there is a very delicate matter that perhaps we should discuss."

Sue sat back down. Peter frowned and wondered what was this delicate matter.

"Religion," Denise began, "it's just that I'm not religious, but Peter is, and the boys' parents were not...."

"It's okay," Peter interjected, "that won't be a problem. I already made up my mind that I would not push the boys towards a belief in God. I will keep my religion to myself."

"Well," said Sue, "that seems to solve that. Now, I should preface anything I say on the matter by stating that I too am not religious. Anyway, if the boys have been brought up not believing in a god, then it would not be helpful,..... no, it would be pretty disastrous, if they were now to be told that there is a god, that what their parents told them was all wrong. We are trying here to preserve as much familiarity in their lives as they had before."

"That will not happen." Peter was emphatic.

"There's nothing stopping you, in the future, saying to the boys, look, others don't believe in God, but I'm one of the ones who does. Then you could say that it would be up to them to form their own opinion."

"Yeah," Peter was dismissive, "well, in the future, as you say. We'll see."

After Sue Hobbs had left, we checked on the children. Thankfully, all three were asleep. This day had to happen. Now it was over. The healing process could begin.

"We'd better have that talk," Denise said, looking rather seriously at me.

"Right, I'll open a bottle of wine, then."

I selected a wine I had been saving. It was a lightly oaked Pinot Noir from Chile. I have become aware that oak and Denise do not sit happily together. However, when I set the bottle on the table, she didn't even look at it. I could see she wanted to get down to business.

"Well," she started the ball rolling, "you heard what Sue said."

I nodded as I poured us both a glass.

"Peter, I'm prepared to commit to you, if you are prepared to commit to me." Denise looks searchingly at me.

"Yes...well...so am I. Prepared to commit to you."

"Yes, but, Peter, I'm prepared to commit to you, but not *just* for the sake of the boys. D'you understand?"

"Yeah...I do."

"What I'm saying is, even if the boys were not here, I would be prepared to commit to you."

"Hmmm...but the boys are here."

"Forget the boys for a minute. If the boys had never entered the scene, I would have been....I mean, ...Oh, I can't find the words. I would want to be with you, even if the boys were not a factor. That's what I'm saying."

Peter sat back and sipped his glass. It was several moments before he spoke again, but then, words never came spontaneously from Peter. They were always measured.

"Denise, I never had a girlfriend....partner....well, I never had anyone in my life before like you."

Denise was on the edge of her seat wondering what he was going to say next. She need not have been worried.

"And…well…I have grown to really like living with you. Yes, I know the boys threw us together. And I'm glad you said what you just said before I opened my mouth. I was going to say I was committed to you….but, I didn't want you to think that my commitment was just so the boys would have a…..female….a mother in the house."

Next morning Peter was awake early. He needed exercise. A run before breakfast. Before leaving the house he checked in on the three little ones and found them all to be sound asleep. Great start.

He ran his normal ten-kilometre circuit and was about to come through his gate when Tom appeared.

"Well, how's things?" Tom enquired.

"Good. Well, so far. We told the boys yesterday that their mother is dead. That she died of the Covid."

"And?"

"Well, there was, understandably, a lot of weeping. But, sure, it had to be done. And now we are on the recovery path."

"Great."

"We want to augment in the boys a sense of family and home. We have this girl, Helina, that I told you about. She arrived yesterday. You must come and meet her. So, we have this house, the garden, and all the people in our home. We have the dog. And you, Tom, we value your friendship and your part of our home. The boys like you, and I want to ask you to come in as often as you can. Will you do that? You don't have to ring or make any arrangements. Just come in. As if you were a grandfather."

"I will, to be sure," came Tom's delighted response, followed by him repeating the word *grandfather*. He seemed to me very pleased with that.

Then Tom told me about his forthcoming marriage to Kevin. Would we come to it? Of course. And Kevin was going to be another resident on our lane. I casually asked why marriage, now. He said he had been wanting to marry Kevin for ages, but Kevin never seemed to be enthusiastic about it. Didn't want to draw attention to them as a couple. Still apprehensive about being pointed out as homosexual. But, now Kevin wanted to formalise their relationship. Put it on a legal footing. Mainly so that he could leave his house in town to Tom.

"You wouldn't think of marrying Denise, would you," he asked, "I mean, wouldn't it help cement this idea of home and family. Now, don't get me wrong, I know you always spoke of being a bachelor all your life, and I don't know the depth of your relationship with her, but I see Denise with them boys, and she's really good with them. I have to say, I was a bit wary of the woman at first, but, now that I have gotten to know her, well, Peter, she's a fine woman, and a lovely person."

Well, that put thoughts in my head, I can tell you. Marry her! I never, for one minute, considered ever marrying. Anyone. I liked my life as it was. I have my job, my house, no appendages. Free to travel where I want, and for how long as I want. Marrying would just tie me down. And if Mary hadn't died I'm sure I'd still be that way. But, she did die. And I have been thrust in as guardian, no, substitute father, to her orphaned children. Like it or not.

Yes, I *liked* my life as it *was*. 'Cause it's all changed now. Actually, I am getting used to having others in the house. I used to get annoyed when the children ran around the place, screeching, knocking over things, breaking crockery, dropping food on the floor. I used to feel a sense of intrusion from Denise, and others, using my bathroom, fiddling with my things, even opening up my laptop. But, I feel myself mellowing. Maybe it's Denise who is causing this mellowness in me. Sex! Well, before I met Denise sex was something that might happen, or might not, generally not, and it never bothered me if and when it did. But now, well, it happens every other night, or morning. And, I have to say, I kinda like it. Denise and I, or maybe I should confine this to just myself, have gotten used to each other's bodies. I know what to do now. Before I was awkward, inexperienced, worried that I would get it all wrong.

When two people do something, y'know, illicit, no, sinful, well, not really that either, intimate, something they can never tell anyone else about, y'now, well anyway, they share a secret, and that secret cements them together more. Well, that's the way I feel about sex anyway. Sleeping with a woman changes a man; you are more careful about your hygiene; you suppress the fart that you would otherwise just let loose; you get in and out of bed quietly, so as not to wake her. Why, I seem to sleep more peacefully with her beside me. Dunno why. She snores. But it is a soft, gentle purr, rather than a snore. Soothing.

Marry her? Perhaps. I'll think about that a bit more. And what would she say? I suppose she'd be happy with it. But maybe she'd turn me down. You can never be sure. She said she was prepared to commit to me. Does that also mean a formal marriage? Did she divorce that Johnny fellow? So, can she actually marry at all? Does she still have thoughts about getting back with him? Would the Catholic Church even allow me to marry her? A divorced woman (if she is divorced at all).

I really have to get my head around my faith. It has been on shaky ground for some time now. Here I am thinking of marriage, with a divorced (hopefully) atheist, bringing up two boys outside the Church, against the wishes of my parish priest. And I haven't been to confession for, what is it, heading for two years. I could talk to Tom about it. He has been my mentor since I was a child. But, sure, I know his attitude. He's a staunch atheist. I could talk to Denise, but she'd be the same. No, this is something I have to work out for myself.

Paul

In late May and early June the world began to return to normal. Covid restrictions were lifted in every country. Freedom. No more masks, no one looking for vaccination certificates. The pandemic is over. It's history. And everyone, suddenly, wanted to go on holiday. Get out of Ireland. A fortnight in the sun.

Me and the lads were thinking of a week in Spain or Portugal. Golf, mar yea, but essentially a week on the tear. We agreed that Johnny would go away and see what he could organise. Johnny's good at that sort of thing.

"Let's play a round of golf on Saturday and we'll have a barney over a pint afterwards," he said.

Yeah, we had the round of golf, alright, and a good few pints – jaysus, I think I knocked down seven or eight. Now, Johnny Dwyer is a character: he speaks with a drawl; remind you of John Wayne; but he's fairly down-to-earth, y'know, a fellow with his head screwed on; and his language is flowery. Johnny tells us to forget about goin to Spain or Portugal, or anywhere else. Here's what he said.

"Look at the chaos at Dublin Airport. Every fucker in Ireland wants to get out. Queues a mile long. Turn up three hours before the flight. And cheap flights me arse. The two airlines, Ryanair and Aer Lingus, are charging big money for tickets. Fleecing us, the bastards. And when I looked up hotels, well, it seems every place, even in the arsehole of nowhere, is booked. No, lads, forget about going abroad for a while."

So, the three of us agreed we'd abandon the idea. And we continued drinking. Paddy was on the Heineken, but Johnny and I were drinking Guinness. Poor auld Paddy just couldn't keep up with the two of us.

"Your turn," Johnny said, pushing his empty glass over.

"Ah, jaysus, give us a chance," Paddy protested, "If I don't finish this one, I'll be two pints behind."

"Paddy," I says, "we don't give a shit how many you're drinking, just go and get us new ones."

We had a right good session that night. But the next morning I was feeling a bit groggy – tightness in the chest, sore head. Now, mind you, the sore head wasn't from the drink. I don't get hangovers, no sir. I'm a seasoned drinker. So, Sheila tells me to take a test. She said there were plenty of antigen kits on the window cill. I didn't bother and went to work. But, sure I just got worse during the day. Runny nose and no energy. I went to bed early.

Next morning I thought I'd better do this test. Well, I suppose Sheila just forced me to do it. Wouldn't ya know it. Fuckin positive. Now, this is the second time I've had it. I thought once you had it, you would be immune. No, Sheila said, you can get it over and over again. So, I was banished to the spare room.

When I came down looking for something to eat, she ordered me out. "Back to your room," she ordered, "I'll bring you something in a while." Then she asked me if I'd contacted the others. What for? To feckin tell them you're positive. I hadn't. I decided to ring Johnny first.

"Johnny," I says, "I have the Covid."

There was silence on the other end of the line. I thought I might have lost him. But, then I heard his drawl.

"I was wondering which fucker gave it to me," he says, "you, ya bollix." I had to laugh.

Paul has been summoned again. Out to Ballyboe to see big brother. Wonder what he wants this time. Maybe apologise for not letting me in last week. Barred. From my own house. By that feckin queer. Perhaps what I said to him sank in and he's going to propose a financial settlement. This fuckin jalopy is becoming an embarrassment. Paul's youngest boy, Shane, has come with him, because Paul has to deliver him to football practice afterwards.

Immediately they entered the drive Shane spotted the football lying in the corner, and he headed for that. Right, that'll keep him quiet for a while.

"Howareya," was Peter's acknowledgement that he had come, "we'll go in the garden and talk." And big brother set off around the house, little brother trotting at his heels. When they reached the lawn Peter turned and spoke.

"You're going to get a letter from the solicitor, probably tomorrow or the next day."

"Yeah?" Well, what was I to think? Solicitor? What have I done?

"Yeah, it seems Mum made a will after all." Now, you're talking. Am I rich?

"The will is a repeat of father's. If she died before him everything went to him, if he died first the house to remain in the Sheridan name. You know the rest."

Shit. No pay-out then. Paul was disappointed. But then Peter put a smile on his face.

"There is a bit of good news."

"Yeah?" He's going to pay me off.

"Our mother had an insurance policy. Something I didn't know about at all. There is an amount that becomes payable on her death."

Well, get on with it. How much am I getting?

"Yeah?"

"Over a hundred grand," Fuck! Paul was about to jump up in the air, but Peter wasn't finished, "deducting her funeral expenses, and split three ways – you, me and the boys – that would make about thirty grand for you." Well, okay, thirty grand is thirty grand.

"Brilliant." Who'd have thought of it. The old gal hiding a small fortune from us. Now, I can get a car.

"Well, that's how I see it, anyway," Peter cautioned, "but we'll have to wait and see what the solicitor says in his letter. Maybe there's something I'm missing."

It would be just my fuckin luck if there is. So, don't start spending it yet. But, try as he might, Paul's brain started spending it anyway. New car. Put in a new kitchen...

The three children suddenly burst out the back door, shouting and screaming, Stella barking in unison. A very good-looking young woman was with them. The two boys recognised Paul and said a guarded hello.

"Helina," Peter called, "I want you to meet my brother."

The good-looking girl approached. She was tall, maybe in her late teens, tanned, with long hair, wearing a long, colourful dress. She was shy and nervous, but I put her at ease with a smile, and I received a guarded smile in return.

"This is Paul," Peter introduced, "he's my younger brother."

A weak handshake followed. "Nice to meet you, Helina." Helina just nodded.

"Helina was the housemaid for Mary in Ethiopia," Peter continued, "now she is with us, and will be a part of our household." Janey mack, part of the household!

The children wanted to play, and they begin to drag Helina with them. She put her hand on Peter's arm and apologised, saying she has to go with them.

Jaysus, didya see the way she put her hand on his arm? She's asking for it, I tell you. But, I know big brother. He just doesn't see it. You'd have to spell it out for him. The girl fancies you.

The eldest of the two boys saw Shane kicking his football in the drive and ran off to him. As the others disappeared down the garden Paul kept his gaze on the girl. Nice figure. Be alright for a night. Maybe *I* could charm her, if he hasn't a mind to.

"Now, I want to talk to you about the boys," Peter interrupted his train of thought, "well, I should say Denise and the boys."

"Yeah?"

"We told the boys that their mother died."

Well, of course she did. Weeks ago.

"She died in hospital in Ethiopia of Covid. Just a few days ago."

"Eh? But, I thought…"

"Never mind what you thought. Mary was being held in prison by the Tigrayans. She had been arguing with them and they arrested her. Whilst she was in prison she contracted Covid. And she died from the Covid."

"But…"

"You can now go and tell your contact in the Westmeath Examiner what really happened."

Jaysus. I told Paddy that she was murdered by the soldiers. What's all this? Can't go and tell him now that I was wrong.

"You told me she was murdered."

"No, I did not. I told you the soldiers had arrested her. We thought she was dead. But, it turns out she wasn't. They were merely holding her."

"Oh, okay….. is her body being brought home, then?"

"No. The Ethiopian government forbids it. Because she died of Covid. But, we are going to have a ceremony to mark her passing. That will be next week. I'll let you know. Now, … Denise and I are going to be married."

Peter stopped momentarily to let that statement sink in.

"I see…" Well, I didn't know whether to congratulate him or not. What was going through my head was what would be the implications for me.

"Then Denise and I are going to formally adopt the boys as our sons."

Another pause to allow the second statement to be absorbed.

"There will be a ceremony for that as well. Oh, and you may as well know that there will be a second wedding in Ballyboe soon."

"Yeah?"

"Tom is going to marry his partner, Kevin."

"Eh?"

"Tom Draper," Peter pointed towards the fence, "is going to marry Kevin McDonald. A same-sex marriage."

Well, fuck that. Two queers are gonna get hitched. In Catholic Ireland! Jaysus, what's the world coming to? Hope I'm not expected to go to that.

Denise

It is early morning. The rays of the sun are effulgently passing through the vertical blinds and onto the bedspread. Another warm day has been forecast. The unusual heatwave that has swept over Europe looks set to continue. Yesterday Ireland experienced its highest temperature ever. The day was spent bringing the hose around the garden, watering shrubs and plants. Great fun for everyone; water sprayed all over the place; children screaming; children wanting to be allowed to take the hose head; Stella barking; Peter protesting at being drowned, yet content to being the victim; took the boys minds off their grief.

Denise is awake, but Peter sleeps peacefully beside her. She looks over at the clock and sees that it is just after seven. She can hear the children downstairs. I told them to leave Helina alone, to let her sleep. Tenen will be asking Omer if it's time yet. Omer will be concentrating on something he is doing, and he will ignore his brother. But Audrey will look at the clock and tell Tenen that there is another twenty minutes. Denise has told them that nobody is allowed to come into her and Peter's bedroom before seven-thirty, and no one should make any noise before that. The dog is to remain outside. I heard the three of them one day last week. They were outside our door, whispering. Tenen asked if it was time yet, and Omer said no, there was another fifteen minutes. So Tenen whispered "let's go in and wake them anyway." To which Audrey said loudly "No."

"Little children often burst into grown-up bedrooms," Denise had told them, "but you three are no longer little children. You are now two young gentlemen and a young lady. Gentlemen and ladies do not burst into other people's bedrooms. They always knock first; wait for the person in the room to say that it's okay to come in, and then they may enter."

The best time for us to have sex is in the early morning. Generally at night we are too jaded from the activities of the day. Perhaps we have had a glass or two of wine. In any case, all we want to do is collapse and sleep. That means that any lovemaking has to be confined to the early mornings, before the children become active. Ordinarily sex is not something that preoccupies my man, but I need it. And, if there is the possibility, no matter how slight, for a little boy or a little girl to come into the room, Peter just won't make any effort. There I am trying to arouse him, and his ears are cocked for noises. The least thing and I've lost him.

This is an old house; the floorboards squeak when you walk over them; so, if a little boy is on his way to our room, we hear him. Well, at least Peter does. The doors are old, and the locks have no keys. They have long ago been lost. So, I went into town the other day and bought a new lock, complete with keys. It took me several hours to fit it. Now, I thought, he need never fear of any interruptions. But even the security of a locked door apparently isn't enough. And yesterday the key went missing. I asked them who took the key. Omer says it was Tenen, but he doesn't remember if he did, and where he might have left it. Luckily the shop gave me two keys. So, I have put the second key on a hook high up on the wall inside the door.

I refer to Peter now as *my man*. Did I tell you that he asked me to marry him last night? I was a bit surprised. Not really flabbergasted, but I definitely didn't expect it. The customary way for a man to ask a woman to marry him is for him to fall on one knee and produce a ring. Not our Peter! It was as if he was trying to negotiate a business deal. He went through the various advantages; if we got married it would be simpler for us to adopt the boys; since we had both committed to each other, then perhaps getting married would formalise that. Formalise! You'd think he would have mentioned the word *love*; that he would say that he had fallen for me. Not at all. Well, anyway, I said yes and gave him a passionate kiss. I'll take him as he comes. I'm actually getting used to, and beginning to love, his little idiosyncrasies.

Helina is settling in well into the house. She has her own room, next door to the boys. She and Audrey are gelling along very well. Audrey looks up to her, wants to see her clothes and things. Wants to try on Helina's dresses. But, I get the feeling that Tenen would like Helina for himself. Last night she took the three of them to bed for the first time. Read them all a story. That was great. It allowed Peter and I some time together. Of course, when we talk the main topic is always the kids; we relate little amusing stories about them, what they said, how they are interacting; although last night our discussions centred on any signs from the boys of their losing their mother.

It is very plain to see that Helina is infatuated with Peter, who, as you might imagine, is totally oblivious of it. She is not as warm to me as she is to the others in the house. Possibly she might resent the fact that I am with Peter, not her. I am in her way, as it were. Anyway, I don't have any worries on that score; I know that my man's eyes will not wander; he wouldn't be aware of Helina's feelings for him, and he'd be mortified if I told him. I pretend not to notice Helina's eyes glistening when Peter approaches, when she wants him to take part in games with her and the kids. She'll get over her infatuation, I have no doubt.

Now that Peter has proposed, I think I'll suggest to him that we sit the children down and that we tell them that Peter and I would like to become their new mum and dad, and what would they think of that. Now, I'll have to have a long talk with Audrey first; she has a dad, albeit one who neglects her. But, he is her father, and I will have to be very tactful in approaching the subject. I'll have to ring Johnny and talk to him too. It would be lovely for us all, me, Peter, Audrey, Omer and Tenen, to formally commit to being a family; brothers, sister, mother and father.

And, when all of our new family is finally established, settled and operational, then I will broach my desire of having another baby. I can only imagine how this will hit Peter. He keeps talking about himself as once a confirmed bachelor, and now, suddenly he has a big family, not just one baby at a time over several years, but a fully formed three-child unit, and with a housemaid thrown in for good measure. He doesn't realise that I too am quite suddenly the mother of, not one, but three children. Actually, I am pre-empting the whole thing! I have stopped taking any form of contraception. If it happens, it happens! Won't be much of a shock to him, will it?

Sue came back yesterday and talked with the boys for some time. But there was an incident with Stella that I can't help finding amusing. Sue had wandered outside with Omer, and they were chatting away. Next minute Stella came over. The dog was wagging her tail. Well, Sue just stood there fossilised. She couldn't speak, couldn't move, and poor Omer didn't understand. Luckily, I was looking out from the kitchen window and saw the whole thing. So, I rushed out and sorted the matter.

Afterwards Sue said she was very pleased with the boys. In her opinion, they had taken their mother's death quite well, but she cautioned that it was early days yet. She said she suspected that Omer already either knew, or had an inkling, that his mother died, not of Covid, but at the hands of the soldiers. However, it seemed that, even if it was the case of a violent death from Tigrayans, he wanted it to be Covid, because Covid was more acceptable in his little mind than the alternative.

Last night I indulged Audrey by listening and joining in one of her fantasies. All of her dolls are now mothers, and the little Lego people are their children. Good mothers have stars that they carry around with them. These stars protect the mothers from death. The stars provide the mothers with a form of mortal immunity. The more stars they have the more immune they become. But one of the mothers has only one star, and this mother is troubled. That part of the fantasy was fine. But the following part was a bit disturbing. This particular one-star mother prayed, and by praying, she became a better mother, and she somehow was rewarded with a second star.

I didn't ask the obvious, pray to who. But two things struck me: all the talk of deaths recently has made Audrey afraid for me, that I might die; obviously she hears talk in school about praying to God, and the concept of praying is seen as a good thing. I suppose this is just a thought that she will lose, but I am concerned.

Living in the country is so much better than in the town. Out here in Ballyboe we have a wealth of wildlife, especially birds. High in the sky we often have buzzards. Tom told us they have a nest in the woods nearby. And they are breeding. We have magpies, finches, robins, wrens, tits, blackbirds, all of them nesting in and around the house. As dusk falls out come the bats, whizzing around the house. I often sit outside watching the activity. Early in the season the magpies built a nest in the whitethorn. When the eggs were laid a jackdaw invaded and made off with one of the eggs. Well, I think it was a jackdaw. Either that or a hooded crow. I can't tell the difference. At the time I felt for the magpies, and I wanted to shoo or to throw stones at the jackdaw.

A week or so later the magpies managed to construct a second nest, this time with a roof on it, and they guarded it very well. Now we have two magpie chicks. I was so happy about that. However, I have totally gone off magpies. Yesterday I saw one of them tearing into the flesh of a dead blackbird. It seemed to me that the magpie killed the blackbird, but didn't eat it. The carcass is lying on the grass, with a host of flies around it. Life can be so cruel. I don't know if the magpie killed the blackbird because it was protecting its chicks, or if it was just in a killing mood.

Omer

Tenen and me are very happy. Uncle Peter – from now on we will be calling him Papa Peter – and Denise – we will be calling her Mama Denise – they asked us yesterday if we would like to be their children. Well, I thought we were their children. Since our real mama and papa died. But they want to *adopt* us. That's the word Uncle Peter, ehhh Papa Peter, said. He said that he had no children and he always wanted children. So, he asked me and Tenen would we like to be his children. We said yes, we'd love to be his children. Papa Peter and Mama Denise are going to get married. So, we will all have to get ready for a big day when they get married. And after that, they will ask the government if they can have us as their children. Why do they have to ask the government? Why can't they just say these boys are ours. I don't really understand that.

So, Audrey will be our sister. Will Audrey will be another of Papa Peter's children? But she already has a father. Can you have two fathers? When we told Tom about it, he said that I could still marry Audrey. He said that boys can marry sisters if they are stepsisters. Not sure what that means. Anyway, I don't want to marry Audrey. I think Tom was just joking.

I'm not sure that Tenen understands what's going to happen. He was asking me afterwards.

"What's a stepsister?" he said.

"It's like a sister that isn't a real sister," I said.

Tom told us that he too was going to get married. And maybe the two marriages will be on the same day. Tom is going to marry Kevin. He's a really old man, older than Tom. We met him yesterday and he's nice. But his hand shakes all the time. When he is drinking something he holds the cup with both his hands. I was never at a marriage between two men before. We went to a marriage in Ethiopia when Amare's brother got married. But he married a girl.

The friend of Mama Denise, the one named Sue, was here the day before yesterday. She loves to chat with me. She tries to chat with Tenen, but he is not a chat person. I heard her asking him about Mama and Papa. That's Mama Mary and Papa Amare. He didn't answer her. But he looked at me, and I answered her. I said that we were sad that our Mama and Papa had died, but that everyone dies at some time. And now we are lucky, because we have a new mama and papa.

Can you believe she's afraid of Stella. Scared stiff of the dog. I was trying to tell her that she doesn't bite, that you could open her mouth with your hands and she would let you. I even can put one of her biscuit bones in my mouth and Stella will take it so gently.

Tenen and me are also very happy to have Helina with us. We love Helina. And she brought us nice necklaces with our names on them, in Amharic. But Helina didn't know who all the people were. So, she asked me, and I told her. She wanted to know if Denise and Sue were Papa Peter's wives. I laughed. She seemed to be surprised when I told her that Denise was going to marry Peter. Helina is now sleeping in the room next to ours.

It was funny yesterday when Tom and Kevin came. Tom had come to show Mama Denise how to make potato cakes. We all sat around the table watching. Me, Audrey, Tenen, and Mama Denise. Papa Peter was not watching. He was talking to Kevin. Tom got a big bowl and crushed potatoes into it. Then he put in all sorts of things – I remember there was a chopped up onion, and egg, but I can't remember the rest. Mama was writing it all down – how much of this and how much of that. When Tom had mixed everything he mushed it up. Then he had flour on his hands and he lifted what was in the bowl and started slapping it around. This was the funny part.

He held up the ball of stuff and he said, "now we have to slap arse."

"What?" said Mama Denise. And we all laughed and wondered what he meant.

"Well," Tom said, "you have to think of this ball of dough – that's what he called it - as a little boy's backside. The little boy has been bold. So, we have to slap his arse."

Tom slapped arse for a while, then he got out a roller and rolled the ball into a big, flat slab. And he cut it with a special cutter into small circles. Then Tom took what was left of the dough and he gave me and Tenen and Audrey a piece each. He told us to mush it and slap its arse. It was funny. I asked Tom if it had to be a little boy's arse, and he said, no, that it could be a little girl's as well. Audrey screamed, "no, only a little boy's."

I got three potato cakes out of my dough, but Audrey only got two, and Tenen made a mess of his. So, Tom helped Tenen, but they only got one potato cake out of his. Afterwards we ate the potato cakes. I ate my three and Audrey ate her two, but Tenen only had one. He was complaining.

"That's not fair," Mama Denise said, "you should have given Tenen one of yours," But I had already eaten the three. So, Mama Denise took one that Tom made and gave it to Tenen.

Tom and Kevin brought us a book, and then Tom sat down with us to read it. It's a really funny book. It's got words like *poo* in it. It's called *The Danger Gang*. There is this boy called Franky Brown. And a girl called Katy Speck. And Franky Brown has a friend whose name is Eric. And there are other boys and girls in their gang. Audrey and me were sitting on the side of the chair listening and looking at the book. But Tenen was just sitting on the floor listening. Some of the words are big, but mostly they're small. Audrey and me could read the big words. Audrey is a good reader. But I think I'm also a good reader. Tenen can't read at all. Tom says he will read more of the story next time. I said he should come and read to us before we go to sleep. Maybe he will. I hope he does.

Yesterday too, Uncle Paul came with his boy. The boy's name is Shane. I think he's ten. I don't think Papa Peter likes Paul. But Shane is nice. He's a really good footballer. Better than Tony, anyway. He told me that he plays in the town league. He plays in the mid-field. Papa Amare was very interested in football, but Papa Peter isn't. Neither is Mama Denise. But girls are never interested in football. I used to play football with Papa Amare. And we sometimes watched it on the telly.

Shane asked me which team do I support.

"I haven't got a team," I told him, "but Papa Amare had a team, but I can't remember the name of it."

"Was it Manchester City?"

"No, that wasn't the one."

"Manchester United?"

"No."

"What about Liverpool?"

I thought it might have been Liverpool, but I wasn't sure. Anyway, I said it was Liverpool.

"I support Manchester City," Shane said, "they won the league this year, and last year."

"Did Liverpool win the league any year?" I asked.

"Well, Liverpool were second this year and last year. And Liverpool won the FA Cup and the League Cup. So, they're nearly as good as Manchester City."

I'm going to support Liverpool. Shane has a big set of football cards. He showed them to me. On each card there is a picture of a footballer, and it tells you which club he plays for and his age, and other stuff. Shane showed me the card of one footballer, whose name is the same as the man Tom is going to marry. Kevin. But I can't remember the last name. Shane said he was the best player in the league. He plays for Manchester City. I'm going to ask Mama Denise and Papa Peter if I can get some of those cards. And, I'm going to ask them if I can go to football practice next time with Shane. Shane said that, if I come to his house, he and me could watch recordings of *Match of the Day*. I think Papa Amare used to watch that. Maybe Tony will decide to support a team. Then he and me can have football cards, and we can swap cards.

"Who's the best footballer for Liverpool?" I asked Shane.

"Oh, that would be Mo Salah," he said, "Mo Salah is the League's top scorer. He won the golden boot for the last two, or maybe three years."

"Mo? That's a funny name. And what is this golden boot?

"Yeah, Mo. You get the golden boot when you are the top scorer. Here, I have his card."

Shane showed me the card for Mo Salah. He has a big smile on his face. "He's from Egypt," Shane said, "that's in Africa."

Mo Salah from Africa. The same continent as Ethiopia. That's great. He will be my number one footballer.

Helina

How my life has changed! Only a few months I was a poor girl in Lalibela. Wearing old and torn gabis, and stitched moccasins. Now I am a young lady in Ireland. Wearing dresses and suits, and high-heel shoes. Learning to be a secretary.

I wrote Inati a long letter three weeks ago, and this morning the postman brought her letter back to me. She is very happy for me. And she was very happy for the fifty-euro Irish bank-note I was able to send to her. She blesses me and wishes me well. She never could believe that the money would get to her. She was sure somebody would know it was in the envelope and would steal it.

Inati told me that there is talk about the war coming to an end. They are talking about a peace between the government and the Tigrayans. But she says that there will be another problem with the Eritreans. Their soldiers came in to fight the Tigrayans, and now they will not go home. Perhaps the government and the Tigrayans will have to join together to fight the Eritreans.

Inati says that Anwar, my brother, is very jealous that I am in Ireland. She gave him my letter and he read it many times. He wanted to write back to me, but Inati said no. She told me that Anwar wants to come to Ireland and live with me. He would give anything to be able to come. I did not know that Inati knew about the schemes and tricks Anwar plays on tourists who came to Lalibela. But Inati told me she found out. She was watching him. He would not tell her where he was getting the money he had. He even bought a new mobile phone. One day when he was out of the house, she got his mobile phone and she was able to read some of the messages and emails he was sending. His new trick is to tell the foreign people in his emails that he has been captured by the Tigrayans, and he is going to be killed unless he can get money for them. My brother is such a liar and a cheat. God will surely punish him for these things.

I have a best friend here in Mullingar. Her name is Olga, and she is a refugee like me. She came from Ukraine where there is also a war. Like me she had to leave because the Russians came into her town. But she is here with her mother and two brothers. Olga and me, we sit beside each other in the secretary school. And on Saturdays we always meet in the town and have a coffee and a talk. When we are walking in the town there are many boys who are looking at us. Some of them want to talk to us. They want to buy us a drink. Olga does not want to do that, and I also don't want to. I was in Olga's house last week. It is a small house, not as big at my house here in Ballyboe. She has a brother. His name is Dmitri, and he is very nice. I think he likes me, and I like him.

Olga and me we have mobile phones. We are texting each other all the time. And there are other girls who go to school, and we text them. And we can send photographs with the mobile phones.

I go to school two times every day. In the mornings I am learning English, and in the afternoons I go to the secretary school. The secretary school is good. Now I can type using all my fingers. Before I was only using two. It was very hard at first. I would be going around thinking in my head QWERT, then ASDF, and then YUIOP and GHJKL. I still can't remember the keys on the bottom row.

I was strange writing to Inati and then reading her letter. Because they were in Amharic. I wonder if I will lose my Amharic language here in Ireland. They have their own language as well. They say it is Irish, but I never hear anyone speaking it. Omer is going to school and he comes home every day with a new Irish word. He said *gura mah agut* to me today, and he said that means thank you.

I am worried that when the war finishes in Ethiopia that I will have to go back, because I will not be a refugee anymore. But Denise told me that will not happen. She is a wonderful woman, Denise. I really like her. And I don't mind that she got Peter. That was only a childish dream I had. But maybe I will get Dmitri!

Audrey and me, we get along very well with each other. She likes to come to my room and talk. We comb each other's hair. And she likes to try on make-up. She will soon be a grown-up young woman.

When I came home last night there was nobody in the living room except Peter. Everybody else must have gone to bed. Peter was sitting at the table with an empty CD case in his hands, listening to piano music. I said hello, but he just grunted something at me. I thought that was strange, but, I didn't say anything else, and said goodnight. Upstairs I saw that the light was on in the bathroom. I thought someone must have left it on. I knocked gently on the door and opened it. I should have knocked and waited. It was very bad of me. Denise was inside. She had a long, plastic thing in her hand. She looked very confused. I was saying sorry and about to close the door when she started speaking.

"You have caught me out."

"Oh, I'm very sorry."

"It's alright. Come in and shut the door." Holding the long plastic thing up, she said, "do you know what this thing is?"

It was a white thing with a small indicator in the middle. Like one of those Covid tester, but bigger. Well, I had never seen one before, so I shook my head.

"It's a pregnancy tester. See the line it shows." She showed the thing to me. "You see this line here," she said, "that means I'm pregnant. Going to have a baby." She had a big smile on her face, so I think she is very pleased about it. "But," she said, with a finger in the air, "it's our secret. For the moment. Don't mention a word to anyone."

I'm confused. She is pregnant. She is happy about it. But she wants to keep it a secret.

"When a woman has to tell a man," she said, "that he is going to be a father for the first time, the announcement has to be carefully planned. You don't just blurt it out. You have to wait for the right moment. Well, you assume he's going to be as pleased as you are, but you never know. So, we won't say anything to anyone. Our secret. When I have told Peter I will tell you."

Denise is the leader in the house here. I see that now. Peter is not as strong as she is. But she never is, what the Irish call, *pushy*. That means she does not order people around. She gets her way quietly. Peter might want to do something that she does not agree with. Denise never insists. And I am always finding it funny that what Denise wants gets done, not what Peter does. That is why I just know Denise will tell Peter this news and he will be pleased about it. Even if it is a shock to him at first.

When I said to Denise that Peter was downstairs listening to piano music and looking sad, she told me what he was doing and why he was sad. She said that Peter was listening to Shoobert. Who is he, I asked. She said this Shoobert lived a long time ago and wrote beautiful music, but he was always poor, because nobody liked, or even knew about, his music when he was alive. The poor man died before he was forty, could never afford to marry, and died of a poor man's disease. Peter says that, if he had been appreciated when he was alive, he would not have been poor and he would not have died so young. He also said that, if Shoobert had lived, he would have been the best composer of all times. I never heard of this Shoobert fellow.

I will tell you a story to show the characters of Denise and Peter.

Peter bought a big car, so that we could all fit in it. We went for a long drive down to a place called Kerry. Peter took us for a walk up a mountain where there was lots of stones that were once a castle. He said it was called Caherconree. On the walk he told us a marvellous story about a king who kidnapped another king's wife and had her in the castle. The good king came to rescue her, and there was a battle. It was a long story.

We were late coming down from the mountain and we stayed in a hotel near it in this Kerry place. We had three rooms; Denise and Peter in one, the boys in another, and me and Audrey in the third. The next morning we had breakfast in the hotel and then we went off in the car. Peter wanted to take us over this pass in the mountains. I can't remember the name of the pass.

When we were going over the pass Peter suddenly found out that we had only a little petrol left. We had to find a petrol station. It was Sunday morning and we were worried that petrol stations in Kerry would not be open. But as we came to the bottom of the mountains we came to a small village and there was a petrol station open. There was a queue in front of us. Peter was driving and he got into the queue. First there was motorbikes and then there was an old man in a van. There was two petrol pumps, but another car was blocking the way to the first pump. After a while the motorbikes went away and the old man in the van moved his car to the second pump. If he had moved it to the first pump we would have been able to go to the one behind it.

Denise said something that I didn't hear, but I think she was complaining that the old man had not moved to the first pump so that he and us could be filling at the same time. But Peter was not concerned. The old man was very slow to fill his van with petrol. He lifted the hose, then he put it back, then he went into the shop, then he came out, and finally he put the hose into the van and filled his tank. Then he went into the shop. We waited for him to come out. But he didn't. We waited more, but he still didn't. I could see Denise getting mad, but I could see Peter didn't care.

Suddenly, and without saying anything to Peter, Denise leaned over and beeped the horn. Beep. Beep. Beep. We waited. They old man was still in the shop. The beeping did no good. Again, suddenly, Denise got out of the car and walked over to the shop. She opened the door and shouted into the shop. When the old man came out we could see he was shocked. He was looking at Denise and he was really afraid of her. I never saw Denise angry before.

Peter began to laugh. Omer asked him why he was laughing and he said, "look at that poor old man. Every Sunday he saunters down to the village to get petrol and buy the paper. Not a care in the world. Sleepy village on a sleepy Sunday morning. Now his Sunday morning is shattered by this English woman."

Omer has a good humour and he could see how funny it was. So could I. We laughed with Peter. Then Audrey and Tenen started to laugh too. But Denise did not think it was funny at all.

"He was in there chatting," she said loudly, when she came back to the car.

Tom

The media was buzzing this morning with the results of the Northern Ireland Census. The headlines read that Catholics now outnumber Protestants for the first time since the founding of the state over a hundred years ago. To an atheist like Tom that news was of little consequence. But when he bought the Irish Times he soon became aware of an even more startling result. The percentage of the population in the North who said they had no religion was seventeen and a half percent, close to double the percentage in the last census. It wasn't simply that the Catholics were having more children than Protestants, rather that both sides were losing their faithful to the no-religion faction. If you were a Protestant you were more likely to lose your faith than if you were a Catholic. The corollary might be that the more educated you were, the more likely you were to lose your faith.

I just can't wait for the results of the Irish Census to appear, but that won't be for another six months.

Ireland is changing before our eyes. In 2015 Catholic Ireland, the country where the Church was more powerful that the State, became the first country in the world to introduce same-sex marriage via a referendum. And the result of the referendum wasn't even close. The Yes vote to legalise same-sex marriage outnumbered the No vote by two to one.

When I was young nobody dared come out as a homosexual. If you were gay you hid it, even from your family. Being gay was about as bad as an unmarried girl getting pregnant. My life was so dismal that I often thought of ending it. If you found another boy to be attractive you were damned careful about showing it. When you associated with other young people you pretended to find girls attractive. Back then we thought of ourselves as somehow dirty, perverted, sinful. There was nobody you could talk to about your "condition".

You might imagine that my being gay pushed me to being also an atheist. Well, I have to say, it certainly helped. I ceased to believe in any god when I was eighteen. I remember talking to a member of the Humanist Society of Ireland, and I boasted that I became an atheist at the tender age of eighteen. His reply was, why did it take you so long?

Throughout my childhood and all the way to middle-age the people of Ireland lived in a puritanical, yet hypocritical society. The Catholic Church was all powerful, whilst their priests were abusing children. Girls who became pregnant were hived off to homes run by nuns, and their babies were sold to Americans.

In 1979 the Pope came to Ireland. I remember shuddering at the sight of thousands, no millions, of people paying homage to him, the biggest crowd ever assembled in Ireland gong to pray with the Pope in Dublin. And those two Catholic celebrities, Bishop Casey and Father Michael Cleary, performing in front of the crowd, worshipped by them. When I think of the transformation that has taken place since those bad old days. First it was revealed that Casey was the father of a young man, and that the Church was paying off the mother, who lived in America. That was in 1988. The country had no sooner recovered from the shock when out came the news that Michael Cleary also had a woman living with him, and a son to boot. Then news began to filter of other priests abusing children. It was scandal after scandal. And me, as an atheist and a gay person, well, I never thought Catholic Ireland would soon become transformed.

I remember in 1986 my disappointment at the failure of the referendum to introduce divorce. And my horror when another referendum put a clause into the constitution that would forever make abortion illegal. But then the scandals began to come out; the Church starting falling from grace, rapidly. Nine short years after the divorce referendum Ireland voted overwhelmingly to legalise it. A complete reversal. In just nine years. And a few years later another referendum removed the 1986 constitution clause and we legalised abortion.

And now look at us! We had a gay prime minister, who's resuming that post again later this year. We have a gay Minister for Children. In the census of 1961 ninety-five percent of the population said they were Catholic, and there was no figure for any atheists in that census. Fast-forward to 2016 and that census shows a drop to seventy-eight per cent Catholic and, wow, we have nearly ten per cent atheist, or no religion. The percentage of LGBT people in society gets higher every time there is a new census. Twenty years ago it was as low at four percent. Now it is thought to be between seven and ten percent.

America seems to be the only country who are not keeping up. Religion there appears to be getting stronger, and polarising people. Why, we even find it odd that some American states are banning abortion. How backward of them!

I'm telling you all this because Peter came over last night. He is still struggling with his faith, poor man. He needs to decide if his marriage to Denise is to be a civil marriage or one in a church. Of course, she's said, no way she is going into any church. Looks pretty certain that they are going the civil route, but the lad still needs to get his head around it. It seems to me that he is in the same mental predicament that I was in when I was young. I couldn't sleep at night because of my sexuality. He can't sleep at night because of his faith. He has to come to terms with the basic matter of whether there is a god, a superbeing, or not. Simple as that. So, he and I thrashed religion, homosexuality, the Catholic Church, divorce, abortion and goodness knows what around for a couple of hours. Old Kevin was basically an onlooker, contributing very little to the debate. Eventually he got tired and sneaked away to bed. I never want to be forthright with anybody, especially

Peter, on these matters. Best to gently make your point and hope that it eventually sinks in.

The weddings look set for September. Or maybe early October. You have to wait for three months after applying for it. The Council will appoint a *solemniser*. Did you ever hear the like of it. Solemniser. We will be having two ladies as our witnesses, that'd be Cora and Georgina, and Peter and Denise will be having two men, Denise's boss in the wine business, Jerome, and that brother of Peter's, Paul. Now, I can tell you, I'll not be fraternising with that fellow. Kevin says I should put it behind me. Just like Ireland has changed, I should accept that what's past is past. After all the hurt he gave me? No, sir. He'd want to come on his knees and apologise…..and mean it, before I'll have a civil word for him.

We seem to be settling into a daily routine here in Ballyboe. I get up and make the breakfast. Kevin is usually an hour behind me. Indeed, he sleeps at least twenty percent more than me. He likes something cooked in the morning, maybe a boiled egg, a rasher and a potato cake, a few sausages. Me, well, I'm a muesli and toast person. We have barely finished our breakfast when the three children come in, Omer, Audrey and Tenen. Oh, and Stella at their heels. They always come together. No matter what we are having they want some of it. So, when I cook I always make some extras for the kids. Peter and Denise mustn't be feeding them properly at all.

In the mid-morning the Ethiopian girl, Helina, comes in. Now, it wasn't my idea. Kevin feels guilty that he's doing nothing around the house, that I am having to cook all the meals, wash up, do the laundry. So, since he is flush with money, and since the girl needs a bit of help, he decided to ask Peter if we could employ her for an hour or two in the mornings. Best idea Kevin ever had. She's a great little worker. Cleans things and places I wouldn't dream of. You should see her ironing. The speed of her. I never bothered with an iron myself, but Kevin likes to look smart. And she's delighted with the money she gets.

The other day Omer couldn't stop talking about football. I told him we call it soccer. I also told him that when he goes to school all the lads in his class will be playing Gaelic, either football or hurling, and he might find himself to be the odd one out. He seemed very disappointed and a little confused about that. I'm sure he believes that football, soccer, is the universal game, and why would that not be the case in Ireland. He'll soon learn.

Kevin came in to the house yesterday. He had been outside with the boys kicking football. At his age! Well, I suppose he was only refereeing. He sits down at the table and starts, "y'know, them gassons have no decent place to kick a ball. Their garden is not flat, and there are too many shrubs and flowers that can get damaged."

I looks at him blandly, not sure what he is telling *me* for.

"That field you have," he says, pointing out the back, "that'd make a great football pitch."

"You mean my corncrake field?" I can't believe that's what's in his head.

"Corncrake me arse," he says, "you'd want to cop yourself on. There's as much chance of corncrakes coming here as there is pigs flying. You've been waiting for the blessed corncrakes half your life. And all we have are a few in the remote islands in the west. Lookit, time you got realistic. You're always pratin on that things have to be plausible. Cut the feckin grass for the gassons. Anyway, if there was some movement of the corncrakes infiltrating from the west, you could always allow the grass to grow agin."

He's right, of course. But, I can tell you, it took me a while to come to terms with it. Giving up a dream I have kept for decades. No point in having unrealistic dreams. Have to deal with the world as it is. Not as you'd like it to be. So, tomorrow, or the next day, whenever the weather is dry, and the grass is dry, I'll sharpen me scythe and start cutting. Haven't used me scythe for years. Looking forward to it. The sweep of the blade, the way you drop the cut grass in a neat row. I've seen many a man make a hames of it.

So, I decided to tell Kevin I was agreeable.

"Tell you what," he said, "we'll call it the Corncrake Field, or even the Corncrake Pitch, the Ballyboe Corncrake pitch. How's that?"

"Right so. We'll tell the gassons. And we'll tell them we need help. They'll have to rake off the cut grass. And I'll make goalposts for either end of the pitch."

"Would that be Gaelic goalposts or them soccer ones?" Kevin asked with a smile.

"Ah, the uprights won't be any harm. So we'll put up Gaelic ones."

Peter

Two boys lose their parents in the war in Ethiopia. Their uncle applies to adopt them. Should be simple and straightforward. That was how Peter saw it. Not on your nelly. Officialdom steps in. The Irish Adoption Board asks for prove of death. If this cannot be furnished then the boys are deemed not available for adoption. No good just stating that the parents are dead – you have to have proof. Affidavits by Helina and, if we could get them, by others in Ethiopia, would be of little use. And we may have tripped ourselves up by telling everyone that Mary died of Covid, when she was actually murdered. Because the Ethiopians have a record of all those who died of Covid. You can imagine the response to a request that the Ethiopian Government confirm the death of Mary and Amare. No reply. Even when diplomatic channels are used, and a reply comes, months later, it is non-committal. Typical: they keep a record of those who died from Covid, but not those who died in their war. So, without proof of death, all we can do is apply for guardianship.

Now that might also sound easy. But, to be deemed suitable for guardianship one has to apply for a certificate. A Declaration of Eligibility and Suitability, no less. You'd think that would be just a formality. Not on your nelly. We are still going through the motions of that, and we have no idea when it will come. Sue is working on it for us. The plan is to have a ceremony on the day we get married for the boys to be confirmed in our guardianship. But if we don't have the Declaration we won't be able to do that. Once we get the Declaration we will have to wait, possibly several years, before we can apply to the courts for adoption, on the basis that the parents are dead, or presumed dead. We won't tell the boys any of this. No point getting their little heads confused. As far as they are concerned, we are their new parents.

I find it just wonderful, that you are sitting at the table, having an after-meal conversation, what the Spanish would call a *sobre mesa,* when a little boy, or sometimes a little girl, pushes themselves in and hikes themself up on your lap. And it is done so naturally. As if this was a common, everyday occurrence. I have this little head in front of me. And, in the case of the boys, I can't help thinking of Mary, my lovely sister. And the child wants to join in the conversation.

Tenen often wants to sit on my lap when I am on the computer.

"Don't touch anything", I say firmly. But he just can't help it. His little fingers reach out to press a button, any button. And he has this devilish glint in his eye.

"Put on something funny," he says.

So, I look on YouTube for a Laurel and Hardy short film. Before I know it Omer and Audrey are also trying to get on my lap. Three little heads in front of me. No chance of me seeing the screen. But, sure isn't it just wonderful.

Tenen is a bit of a showman. He likes to perform, whether it's with his little guitar, or dancing to music, or just joking, or fantasising about something. And it seems that Audrey and Omer, and most particularly Helina, really find him funny. The three of them are hanging on his every word. The little lad likes to boss people. He can't do that with Audrey or Omer – when he's with them they like to be in control. But he loves it when Helina has the time to play with him, because she succumbs. He orders her to do this, and move that, no not that way, and she just does as he tells her. Great patience.

Omer is very interested in chess. He and I often get the chess board out and play. I played him a video from YouTube on *Chess Openings*. But Omer has a concentration time of about fifteen minutes. Then he gets distracted, turns to something else. Sometimes he's in a trance, his little mind off somewhere. And no matter how many times you call him he remains in that trance. He is sitting at the table, and Denise tells him to eat, but he is just staring into space. She spoons the food into his mouth. He eventually comes out of the trance and finishes the food himself.

We were driving the other day in the car, the kids in the back, Denise at the wheel. We were to go shopping in the afternoon, but Omer had asked if he could stay back and play with Tony in Tony's house, and we had agreed.

All of a sudden Denise asks, "have you arranged with Tony and his mum to be in their house this afternoon?"

There is silence. Omer is obviously in another trance. I venture, "I think we can take that as a no."

Just as Denise is about to speak again out comes a weak "yeah" from Omer. I just found it really funny, and couldn't help laughing. Then Denise began to laugh. And she had to stop the car. Omer, I think, realised what had happened, and he joined in.

"Why are we laughing?" Audrey asks.

This day next week, the 11th of October, is the big day. It will all happen in the Park Hotel. Tom and Kevin will be married first. Then it's our turn. After that, assuming the Declaration comes through, the ceremony of guardianship. I pray that everything will go according to plan.

Pray! I'd better tell you something important. Well, important to me. We got these guardianship papers, and Denise filled in most of the forms, then handed the stuff to me. I read through them. When I came to the section on religion, vis a vis the children and the prospective guardians, there seemed to be an added complication if the religion of the latter was different to the religion of the former. Well, I pondered it, put it aside and went out for a walk, met Tom, who gave me an earful about the people in the North of Ireland losing their faith, came back in, and, in reply to the religion of the second guardian, I wrote *no religion.* Well, lookit, I'm getting married to a divorced woman, and an atheist to boot, in a civil ceremony, adopting children who have been brought up as atheists. Sure, I'd be only kidding myself introducing religion into the whole scenario.

Denise and I have not spoken yet about that. I'm not saying I have become an atheist, no. Let's say I'm possibly now an agnostic – unsure. And I haven't spoken to Tom, or anyone else about the matter either. So, it looks like I am, or I will be, one of the statistics of those moving over from Catholic to No Religion, that Tom talked about. That leaves Helina. I really don't know what I am going to say to her. She is used now to me taking her to mass on Sundays. Maybe I'll ask Margaret next door to bring her. I'll have to fooster some reason for it to give to Margaret.

I was contemplating biting the bullet and going to see Father Dunlea. Y'know, waltz up to him and just tell him the story – I'm getting married to a divorced woman, an atheist, in a registry office; oh! and don't expect me in church for a while; maybe don't expect me again, ever. But, then whom should I meet only Missus Simmonds. Problem solved. I don't need to stress myself with Dunlea. Mrs. Simmonds will do handsomely. So, I told her the whole story. Needless to say, she just lapped it up. You could almost see the entries she was making in the notebook in her head. *Oh, I hope you're doing the right thing, Peter*, was all I got from her. Can you imagine the session I would have had with Dunlea. *Would you just sit down with his Grace if I can arrange something with him?*

Oh, I nearly forgot to tell you about the homeless man. Missus Simmonds filled me in. Well, he managed to wangle his way into the Ukrainian refugee crisis, got himself a room in a fine hotel and all. But the Ukrainians flushed him out. Sergei is Russian! And the Ukrainians won't have him anywhere near them. So, he's had to take himself off out of the town.

Omer came home from school last Friday, and he went straight to Denise. I was still at work.

"Mama Denise," he started, "can I ask you a question. But maybe you won't be able to answer. Maybe I'll have to ask Papa Peter."

"What is it, then?"

"Did Mama Mary really die of the virus or was she murdered? A boy in my class said that she was murdered."

Well, Denise decided this matter was too big for her, so she told Omer that, as far as she knew, Mary died in hospital of the virus. But she advised that he should talk to me about it. And then she rang me, so that I would be prepared. And she warned Helina too about it. Leave it to Peter.

When I came home I waited for him to come and talk to me, but he was otherwise busy. So, I volunteered to take them to bed. But still he never took the opportunity of speaking about it. He didn't seem in any way to be troubled, so I didn't raise the matter. No, that was no good, not for Denise. I had to confront the lad about it. My plea to let sleeping dogs lie didn't even register with her. So, after breakfast on Sunday I took him out to the football pitch.

"Denise said that some boy in your school thought your mother didn't die of the virus. Is that right?" I didn't want to use the word *murder*.

"Yeah. It was Mickey Harte. But Johnny Battle was listening, and he thought the same."

"Okay. Okay. Some fool in Ireland made up this story of your mother being murdered. And there was a ransom to be paid for getting you two boys back…"

"Was that what was given to Habtamu? The ransom?"

"Who?"

"Habtamu. He was the one who took us to Addis Ababa. And Hashim gave him a lot of money. I saw him count it. And he wanted more."

My back was against the wall. I felt cornered. Don't panic.

"No, no. Hashim gave that other fellow money for transporting you from Lalibela to Addis. And that fellow, whatever his name is, had to pay the soldiers to let you through. That's all. No ransom. And your mother was in prison, yes, but she got the virus there and they moved her to hospital. But they had no medicine there and she died."

I came away from that boy convinced he found my story highly sceptical. Denise and I talked again about it. She concluded that he probably knew, or suspected, the truth, but he was content to live with the less traumatic alternative. We'll talk to Sue about it.

Life in Ballyboe has settled down. I have a new job; Denise is back at work; she's now driving my car; I had to get a bigger one – for the family; Audrey and the boys are at school; and Helina is also going to school. After nine in the mornings the house is empty for the day. Then, in the late afternoons, it is bustling again.

An old friend of my father's, Pauric Slattery, has asked me to work for him. He runs a travel agency in the town, indeed, the only travel agency in Mullingar. Pauric is in his seventies, and he wants to retire. He wants to hand over the business to someone, and he has no one in the office capable of running it. So he says. I have known Pauric for many years, and I have helped him on occasions. He'd ring me and ask some weird questions about some foreign country that he was not familiar with. Travel agency is a dying business, as far as I am concerned. People can surf the Internet and plan their own travel. The types of clientele we get are either elderly people with no experience of the Internet, or young ones about to get married and with more money than sense, too busy organising the marriage itself. Get someone else to plan the honeymoon. When a couple call and say they want to spend a week in the Seychelles, then hop over to Kenya for a week's safari, and finish off their holiday in Rome, you have to know which airlines to check on, which hotels are available. More importantly, from a business point of view, you have to know what companies will pay you a commission for placing the booking with them.

Denise is back in the Wine Emporium with Jerome. I am helping them with the process of setting up wine tasting evenings. I think I've convinced them that one of the wines we taste should be a mystery bottle. Each of the participants gets a small trickle of a wine, and they are asked to write down what the grape is, where it is from, and the vintage. It really focuses the mind of what you are drinking, and, in my opinion, is a great aid to wine appreciation.

Denise didn't want Helina just to become, what she calls, a skivvy, a cleaner, a domestic. Helina was happy to be doing the housework here and for Tom and Kevin, but we agreed that the girl has more potential than that. So, every morning she goes off to learn English, and then, in the evenings she is attending a secretarial college. She has met a girl of her own age in the English classes who is from Ukraine. And we had to buy her a mobile phone. Despite her sheltered upbringing that young lady has become a woman of the world, a survivor.

Denise is trying to get pregnant. Bit of a shock to me. Still, from zero to three children in a few months, a fourth is going to be neither here nor there. Not to mention a teenage refugee. Will I feel any difference between my adopted children and a child of my own? Don't know.

On the 11th our family – isn't it just great to say that, our family – will drop the Mamas and Papas. From then on it will be Peter and Denise. We had a sobre-mesa debate on it the other night. Audrey was inclined to continue to call her mother Mammy or Ma, but she came around to the notion, and she's happy with it. She even wants her surname to be Sheridan. Since Denise has opted to take the Sheridan name, maybe Audrey didn't want a surname different to her mother's. Or maybe this is an indication of her integration into our family.

We had visitors last Sunday. Denise's ex, Johnny, and his mother, Nan McMahon, paid us a visit. I was watching to see the relationship of Audrey to her father. There was not much between them. Johnny is a charmer, an egotist, loves to be the centre of attention. I found it remarkable how he and Denise continue to have a very friendly relationship. Y'know, you're married to someone, the marriage isn't working, mainly because one of them is sleeping around, you decide to split up, the man never comes near his daughter, but here they are being very friendly with each other. Remarkable. But Nan is a wonderful, compassionate person. And Audrey simply adores her. Twice a week now she spends an hour or two with Nan. And Tenen goes with her. They really enjoy the time with Nan.

Tenen and Audrey get along really well. She seems to mother him. And he likes it. They play a lot with the dolls, much to the disgust of Omer. I'm wondering if Tenen is going to be gay. It wouldn't surprise me if he was. The other day the two of them were rooting through Audrey's big box of Lego. There must be over a thousand pieces in it. She was searching for a particular piece, a very small, round one. Tenen would pick up a piece and show it to her and she would say, no smaller, and it's grey. That little girl knows every one of the thousand or more Lego pieces. I ventured over.

"Can I help?" I asked.

"No," Audrey replied, without even looking up. "Tenen and me will find it. You go back to playing with your computer." Summarily dismissed. By an eight-year-old.

But Omer and Audrey hop off each other. Although he is stronger than her, she is well able to fight her corner. And she protects Tenen from him. Omer can be sitting there reading or doing a puzzle, quiet as a lamb, when suddenly he is up and goes wild. It's like someone came along and gave him an injection. Audrey can see it coming. And she is ready.

The other day I was out in the garden doing some weeding. I heard Tenen roaring crying. Immediately the door opened and out came Omer.

"What did you do to him?" I asked.

"Nothing."

"Then why is he crying?"

"Don't know."

"I'll go in and find out."

"I just gave him a very gentle push." He decided to own up, and get his side of the story in first..

"Show me."

Omer came over and pushed my arm ever so gently. He looked at me.

"That's all I did." Innocence personified.

Tenen's version, corroborated by Audrey, was simply poles apart. "He pushed me hard and knocked me down."

The lad is boisterous. He has so much energy. Find him a field and let him off. Let him release some of that energy. Denise says we should knock the energy out of Omer every evening before bedtime. Let him go out and kick football; tell him to do tend laps of the garden and you will time him; any physical challenge that will tire him out.

What's that song, *He's football crazy, he's football mad, and the football game has robbed him of the little bit of sense he has?* Our Omer if football crazy. He has resisted all attempts at going over to the Gaelic side. No, soccer, soccer, soccer.

I was musing about these censuses that Tom was talking about. They provide us with interesting information on life in twenty-first century Ireland: what religion we follow; our sexual orientation; how many children we have, etc. Wouldn't it also be interesting to find out what percentage of us follow sport. Take me for instance. I do not follow any sport. Denise, likewise. My father and mother were never interested. But our Paul is. Where did he get it from? The man next door to Denise is. Not just one sport, but nearly every sport. And now Omer. Where on earth did his little mind come up with soccer. And not just soccer – Liverpool. Why didn't he choose Manchester United or some other side, maybe an Irish club. No, it's Liverpool. And Tenen is quite oblivious to sport.

Paul brought Shane out on Sunday evening to play soccer. Of course, Paul knows everything about soccer. He had Omer mesmerised. Showed him how some fellow with long hair tied in a bun on his head, called Haaland, headed the ball into the net last week, taught him how to dribble.

I can't have that. My son has to look up to me. I want to be number one in his Superego. So, I have spent hours on the Internet, reading about soccer, looking at the scores, keeping up to date with the Champions' League. Every Saturday and Sunday night I sit down and watch *Match of the Day*. I have a notebook on my lap, writing down names. I record every episode. Then, on Mondays, Omer and I watch the recordings. Liverpool are doing badly this year, but Omer is sticking to them. Loyalty. I will get around to taking him to a live match one of these days. Then, maybe I'll take him over to Liverpool. But it will have to be a game that Liverpool are sure of winning. I'm not taking the kid to see them get hammered by Manchester City or the like.

It was funny last week. I was in Day's Bazaar and I spotted some football cards. I saw that Omer was always looking at them. Well, I couldn't just come home with football cards for him. So I bought a set for Tenen as well, and a set of Pokémon cards for Audrey. Omer was looking through the cards, and he was very thankful for them. Tenen didn't open his. You could tell that they meant little to him. Omer kept asking him to open the packet. When he eventually did, Omer nearly had a fit.

"Oh, you've got a Mo Salah card," he said to Tenen. Tenen looked at the card, but thought little of it.

"Would you like to swap that card with me?" The tone in Omer's voice was so amusing. It was suggesting I'm your loving brother, won't you be kind to me and give me the Mo Salah card. I'd be ever so grateful.

No. Tenen was not going to part with the card. No, he wouldn't take four cards as a swap for it. No, neither would he take two euros. No, not even five euros. I would predict that Tenen will forget about the Mo Salah card eventually, and it will find its way into Omer's collection.

I had to thank Tom for giving over his precious corncrake field as a football pitch. Now the pitch is a haunt for lots of boys in the neighbourhood, who congregate to play. It's great for Omer. All of a sudden everyone knows our Omer and his field. And now Tom's cutting the grass, regularly killing the weeds. Why, the pitch is fully lined out. A proper football pitch.

Tom's response had a note of sarcastic mirth in it.

"Ah, sure, there comes a time in our lives when we have to succumb to the inevitable. Y'know, that belief, or desire, you have been clinging to for half your life, suspecting it to be doubtful, kick it around a bit more, swallow hard, and eventually give in. Face up to reality. In your case it might be religion. In mine it was waitin for the feckin corncrakes."